Twelfth Night

or
What You Will

PAUL ILLIDGE

Creber Monde

In memory of Elyse Schultz (1952-2007)

Published by Creber Monde Entier
265 Port Union, 15-532
Toronto, ON M1C 4Z7 Canada
(416) 286-3988 1-866-631-4440 toll free
www.crebermonde.com
publisher@crebermonde.com

Distributed by Independent Publishers Group
814 North Franklin Street
Chicago, Illinois 60610 USA
(312) 337-0747 (312) 337-5985 fax
www.ipgbook.com
frontdesk@ipgbook.com

Design by Derek Chung Tiam Fook
Communications by JAG Business Services Inc.
Printed and bound in Canada by Marquis Imprimeur, P.Q.

First Printing March 2007

Library and Archives Canada Cataloguing in Publication

Illidge, Paul
    Twelfth night : a novel / Paul Illidge.

(The Shakespeare novels)
ISBN 0-9686347-4-5

    I. Shakespeare, William, 1564-1616. Twelfth night. II.Title.
III. Series: Illidge, Paul. Shakespeare novels.

PR2878.T97I45 2006   C813'.54   C2006-904409-0

Twelfth Night

Text of the First Folio 1623

Characters

Orsino	Duke of Illyria
Sebastian	twin brother of Viola
Antonio	a sea captain, friend of Sebastian
Captain	who saved Viola
Curio	Orsino's personal attendant
Valentine	gentleman attending on Orsino
Sir Toby Belch	uncle to Olivia
Sir Andrew Aguecheek	companion of Sir Toby's
Malvolio	Olivia's steward
First Officer *Second Officer*	serving the Duke
Fabian	servant to Olivia
Feste	clown/jester to Olivia
Olivia	a countess
Viola	Sebastian's twin sister
Maria	maid to Olivia
Servant	to Olivia
Priest	

Nobles, sailors, soldiers, musicians, attendants

His ship having gone down off the coast of Illyria during a storm the previous night, a sea captain orders the four sailors in the wooden lifeboat to pull hard on their oars one last time, then motions for the young woman seated beside him, Viola by name, to lean back as the boat glides in and lurches to a stop on the sand, the sailors quickly shipping oars and jumping out to haul the boat up from the shallow water and onto the beach.

"What country is this, friends?" Viola inquires, gazing at the lush green woods and tree-covered hills beyond the beach.

"This is Illyria, my lady," the captain answers and helps her from the boat onto shore.

She broods for a moment, touching a hand to her wet, bedraggled hair. "What am I doing in Illyria when my brother is in heaven?" she asks sadly. She looks down at her sodden clothes, hanging limp and heavy on her delicate frame. "Perhaps through good fortune he was not drowned. What think you?" she turns to the captain, he and his men lugging several trunks from the boat and setting them down on the sand.

"Well, it was through good fortune that you yourself were saved," he points out as he works.

Viola casts her eyes out to sea, "And so he may have been too," she muses, gazing at wisps of white cloud that hover over the distant blue horizon.

"True, madam," the captain agrees, "and to offer you some comfort in that possibility, I can tell you this: after our ship went down—when you and those few others who were saved clung to our boat in the driving wind—I saw your brother, brave in the face of danger, tying himself to a section of the broken mast that was floating on the water, courage and hope spurring him on in his desperation. For as long as he was in sight I watched him there, battling the waves like the hero in Greek myth who saved himself by riding on a dolphin's back."

She takes a coin from a pouch she has tied around her waist, and gives it to the sea captain. "For your encouraging words, here's gold. My own escape makes me believe he could have as well, and your story encourages me in that hope. Do you know this country Illyria?"

"Yes, madam, I know it well, for I was born and raised not three hours' travel from this very place."

"Who governs here?"

"A noble duke, both in birth and reputation."

"What is his name?"

"Orsino."

"Orsino… I have heard my father speak of him. He was a bachelor then, I believe."

"And still remains one, or was said to be until very recently. For I left here no more than a month ago and then it was being rumored—you know how people gossip about their betters—that he sought the love of the fair Olivia."

"Who is she?"

"A well regarded young woman, the daughter of a count who died some twelve months ago. He left her under the protection of his son, her brother, who died tragically shortly afterward. Because of the dear love she had for him, at least so the rumors have it, she has given up the sight and company of men."

"Oh that I could serve such a lady and keep my plight hidden from the world until I am better prepared to reveal it."

"That would be hard to do, madam, because she will not grant anyone's desire to see her, not even the Duke's."

She considers for a moment. "You seem a decent man, Captain. And though evil can mask itself within a pleasant-seeming face, yet I feel I'm not deceived by your fair looks and well-meaning manner. I pray you—and I'll pay you generously for doing so—help me conceal who I am, and assist me in fashioning a disguise that may suit my purpose. I'll serve this Duke. You can present me as a well-versed young man who could be of valuable service to him in his present circumstance. Whatever may happen I will trust to time, but I ask that you reveal to no one this plan of mine."

"You be his eunuch, and your mute I will be," he vows. "If my tongue makes known the truth, let my eyes no longer see."

"I thank you. Lead on…"

He gives his men the order to move out, points them to a clearing in the trees and, with Viola beside him, leads the way forward….

Morning sunshine streams through the tall windows of the palace's gallery Hall where Duke Orsino, the Count of Illyria, comes every day to paint the landscapes, still life and portrait pictures for which he is quickly becoming renowned: not masterpieces, by any means, but "masterful pieces" according to his aging Florentine teacher Lugozzi, who in his day had personally known Rubens, Rembrandt and even the troubled Italian genius Caravaggio.

But this morning it is Orsino who is troubled. His long brown hair tied behind his head in a ponytail, his fine-featured, aristocratic face is set in a forlorn frown as he stands before his wooden easel and contemplates the oil painting that, for several weeks now, he has been unable to finish. Everything about the work has come smoothly: the high-backed, carved-wood chair in which the woman is sitting, her long-sleeved dress of violet blue, a splendid necklace of sapphires and diamonds radiant against the velvet fabric, the fingers of her slender hands folded elegantly on her lap. Yet where there should be a face, there is but a round patch of unpainted canvas…

On the other side of the hall, under the formal portraits of the Duke's family ancestors, four string musicians are playing their lutes and mandolins softly, supervised by old Curio, the Duke's personal attendant, who has brought the musicians here this morning in hopes that their playing will inspire Orsino to make progress on his painting. A thin man with slightly stooped shoulders, watery blue eyes and silver-white hair combed neatly on his head, he keeps a concerned eye on his master and signals to the musicians to play faster or slower, louder or softer—more joyfully or, as is usually the case now, more sadly—depending on Orsino's reaction to the music.

Seeing his master take up his palette and brushes—apparently to begin work on the painting—Curio casts the musicians an approving smile, though no sooner has he done so than Orsino lets out a bitter cry, throws down his palette and brushes and grabs the woman's portrait off the easel, hurling it in frustration at the nearby wall. The picture bounces off the wood paneling and lands among numerous other paintings of the same faceless woman that are strewn across the floor.

With a quick wave of his hand, Curio stops the music, watching in dismay as Orsino removes his painter's smock, lets it drop to the floor and trudges over to the windows where, when he has regained his composure, he lets out a helpless sigh. Looking over, he catches the worried look on Curio's face. Beside him, the musicians are still holding their instruments, fingers poised over the strings.

"If music be the food of love," Orsino sighs, "play on." Curio signals the players to resume and the soothing strains rise in the hall once again. "Let it fill me until, groaning from excess, I can bear to hear no more…"

Sunlight pouring into the room around him, Orsino's gaze follows a blue and yellow-winged butterfly that has come in through one of the open windows and is now flying at the glass panes in a fruitless effort to escape.

"—There!" Orsino blurts suddenly and turns from the butterfly to face the musicians. "That last strain – could you play it once more?"

"Certainly, my lord," says Curio with an obliging nod and arranges for the melody to be repeated.

"It struck me with such sadness," the Duke explains, "like the hushed sound of autumn leaves rustling in the forest." Coming up behind, he cups his hands gently around the stranded butterfly and guides it to an open window where he releases it and it flutters off outside. He turns abruptly to Curio and the musicians. "—That's enough, for now no more. It's not as sweet as it was before."

All is silent in the large empty hall except for the sound of the Duke's shoes on the polished wood floor as he paces in front of the windows, Curio and the musicians with their eyes trained on Orsino, waiting uncertainly while he gathers his thoughts.

"Oh spirit of love," he pronounces gloomily, "how cruel and all-consuming you are! Your power as vast and boundless as the sea, nothing comes near you, however great or strong it might be, but you pull it under like some small thing of little worth. So over-powering these fantasies of love…illusion and wild imaginings drown all thought and reason, like nothing else on earth…"

"Will you go hunting, my lord?" Curio inquires.

"What, Curio?"

"The deer, my lord."

"Why, so I do." He places a hand over his heart, "with the dearest thing in me. Oh, when my eyes first saw Olivia I thought she purified the air. In that instant I was turned into a deer, and my desires—fiercely cruel hounds—have pursued me ever since."

The gallery door opens and the messenger Valentine enters. A young man about the same age as the Duke, he advances into the room and presents himself.

"Well, what news from her?" Orsino asks.

"So please you, my lord, they would not admit me to the house. But from her gentlewoman I return you this answer: the outside world shall not behold her again until seven summers have passed. Indeed, like a nun within cloister walls she will keep to her chamber, her beauteous face veiled to hide the tears of grief she will daily shed preserving the love she had for her dead brother, which she would keep fresh and lasting in her sad memory."

Moved by Valentine's words, Orsino looks away. "She who can feel such tender and devoted love for a brother… Imagine what her passion will be when mourning gives way to feelings for her one, true love. Come, Curio, let us go and enjoy the garden's magnificence; love-thoughts are best savored amid sweet floral scents…."

Seagulls shrieking ravenously as they circle in the sky above the town, the cobblestone street that runs alongside Illyria's main harbor is busy as men, women and children work to clean up after last night's vicious storm. Not only have the lamplights and shopkeepers' signs blown down, the window shutters on many houses are battered and broken beyond repair. Trees have fallen, wagons lie overturned on the ground, their wheels missing, and crowds of spectators have gathered and are gawking at several fishing boats which the hurricane winds have lifted out of the water and deposited almost on the doorsteps of houses along Merchants Row, the largest establishments in the seaside town: four-storey mansions where the wealthiest traders and ship-owners reside.

Outside the largest of these, a gentleman at the reins of a black, horse-drawn buggy has stopped to commiserate with a stout, well-dressed woman who is surveying the damage done to the garden flowers around her house. Arms folded across her chest, she listens as the gentleman speaks, then shakes her head in dismay and is about to answer him, when a resounding crash goes up from inside the house behind her. She turns quickly, and with one crash following another in quick succession, it becomes clear that someone is trying to break open the shutters of a main floor window, the painted wooden slats beginning to crack and splinter with the force of the blows from inside. More embarrassed than annoyed, the woman promptly excuses herself and heads in-doors, jumping when another loud crash goes up behind the shutters…

Charging through the entry foyer, the woman, whose name is Maria, hurries straight to a set of double-doors and throws them open to behold a large middle-aged man in soiled, wrinkled clothes that look like he has slept in them, hoisting the armchair over his head that he's been throwing at the shutters.

"Don't you dare!" cries Maria, and steps into the parlor, which looks as though it's just been ransacked. Tables, chairs and other pieces of furniture are turned over, paintings are hanging cock-eyed on the walls; scattered on the floor among articles of clothing, blankets, cushions and several pairs of mud-covered boots, are chicken bones, cheese rinds, crusts of bread and numerous empty wine bottles.

The large man, Sir Toby Belch by name, has put down the armchair and picked up his drinking tankard. Maria folds her arms and heaves a sigh of resignation, apparently not surprised by the scene before her.

"What the devil does my niece mean by taking her brother's death this way?" Sir Toby growls irritably, staring down at his bare feet "Too much worry leads to the grave, you know that as well as I do." He lifts the tankard and drinks.

"I know you must come home earlier at night, that's what I know," she scolds. "Your dear niece, my lady, takes great exception to the hours you keep."

"Well, let her make me the exception to her exceptions," he comes back, sets the tankard down and starts rummaging on the floor to find his socks and boots.

"And if she did, would you confine yourself within the limits of proper behavior?"

"Confine?" he demands. "I'll con*fine* myself no more properly then than I do now." He locates his boots, sits down and, amid grunts and burps, puts them on. "These clothes are good enough to drink in, and so be these boots too." He is slow getting to his feet. "—If they be not, let them be *hung* from their own bootstraps." He takes up the tankard again, propping the lid open with his thumb, and drinks off the remaining contents, letting out a satisfied burp when he's done.

Maria has set about straightening up the room.

"This heavy drinking will be your ruin," she warns. "I heard my lady speak of it just yesterday, and of a foolish knight you brought home one night to woo her."

"Who, Sir Andrew Aguecheek?"

"Yes, him."

"He's as good as any man in Illyria," Sir Toby protests.

"Good in what way?"

"In the way of ten-thousand gold ducats a year."

"And all spent within the year too, I don't doubt. He's a simpering fool and a squanderer to boot."

Sir Toby follows behind her as she works. "Shame on you for saying so, lady. I'll have you know he plays the violin-cello, and knows three or four languages off by heart, word for word. And he's been endowed with the finest gifts of nature."

"Indeed, he's a natural-born fool. For besides being a simpleton, he's a great one for quarrelling I'm told, and—if he didn't have the gift of cowardice in running away from his quarrels—it's thought by wiser folk than myself that he'd quickly have the gift of a grave."

"By this hand," Sir Toby bellows, "they are scoundrels and subtractors that say so. Who are they?"

Maria stands at one end of an overturned couch. "Those who say that he's drunk every night in your company." She points for Toby to take the other end.

"Drinking toasts to my niece!" he objects, but helps Maria with the couch. "—I'll drink to her as long as there's a passage in my throat and drink in Illyria. He's a coward and a villain who will not toast my brother's dear daughter till his head starts—" But he breaks off when he sees a lanky young man standing in the doorway, his straight and straw-colored hair hanging limply almost to his shoulders.

"Why, speak of the devil!" Sir Toby exclaims. Here be Sir Andrew Agueface himself."

"Sir Toby Belch! How goes it, Sir Toby?" Aguecheek pushes hair away from his face with a finger—a face powdered with white make-up, which only partially hides his blemished complexion—then moves into the room, making interested eyes at Maria as he passes her. "Good day, my pretty shrew," he says saucily.

"The same to you, sir," she replies and busies herself with straightening a portrait of Olivia and her twin brother that was painted when they were children.

While exchanging handshakes, Sir Toby motions with his head toward Maria.

"Accost her, man, accost her," he urges his young friend.

"What?" Sir Andrew asks, confused.

"My niece's chamber maid." Sir Toby winks and shoves him toward Maria.

Aguecheek takes several steps forward and stops. "Good Mistress

Accost," he declares boldly, "I most desire to know your betters—to know you better," he corrects himself.

"My name is Mary, sir."

"Good Mistress Mary Accost—"

"No, no," Sir Toby takes him by the arm and pulls him aside. "'Accost' means to go up to her, flatter her, take her in your arms and hold her."

"On my life, I couldn't do that with other people looking on," Sir Andrew protests. "Is that really the meaning of 'accost'?"

"Farewell, gentlemen," says Maria and heads for the door.

"If you let her walk away like this may you never call yourself a man again," Sir Toby warns.

The pressure bringing a fretful look to his face, Sir Andrew deliberates briefly then goes. "—If I let you walk away like this may I never call myself a man again!" Maria stops walking and turns, his fervent bravado prompting an amused, slightly mocking smile. "—Fair lady," he says, offended, "do you think you have fools in hand?"

"Not at all, sir, for I don't have you by the hand."

"That is true—but you shall." With an elaborate flourish he offers her his hand.

She studies it for a moment then takes it and strokes the palm. "Well, sir, each to his own opinion," she glances up and meets his eyes with a burning look. "But *I'd* say, bring your hand along to the pantry and let it have a drink…"

"What, sweet lady?" He tries to pull his hand loose, flustered by her suggestive overture, but Maria keeps hold. "What," he fumbles for the words, "—what is the meaning of your metaphor?"

"It's dry, sir," Maria says lightly.

"I would hope so," Sir Andrew snaps. "I'm not such a fool that I can't keep my hand dry." Unable to help herself, she begins to laugh. "But what's the joke?" Sir Andrew turns from her and casts Sir Toby a helpless look.

"It's a play on words, sir," Maria tells him.

He ponders a moment. "You seem full of such plays," he complains.

"Indeed, sir, I have them at my fingertips." She releases his hand.

"But now that I let go the hand, I am all out." She rolls her eyes at Sir Toby and hurries off, Sir Andrew, a blank look on his face, watching the door even after she's gone.

Sir Toby comes over quickly.

"Good Sir Andrew," he commiserates, "you need a good cup of wine!" He pours one for his friend, who with a finger pushes the hair off his face and drinks up. "When did I ever see you so put down?" Toby says.

"Never in your life, I think, unless you've seen wine put me down," Sir Andrew mopes. "Sometimes I think I have no more brains than the most ordinary man. But I'm a great eater of beef," he says, perking up. "Perhaps *that* is what hampers my wits."

"No question about it," Sir Toby agrees as he goes and retrieves his tankard from the table where he set it down. There is a plate piled with chicken bones, bread crusts and cheese rinds beside it. Picking up one of the rinds, Toby makes a sour face when he sniffs it, but brings it with him nonetheless when he returns to Sir Andrew's side.

"Yet if I thought it was the beef," Sir Andrew reasons, "I would swear off it." He looks down glumly, contemplating his wine. "I'll ride home tomorrow, Sir Toby," he says after a moment.

Sir Toby stops nibbling his rind in mid-bite and throws a worried glance at his friend. "But *pourquoi*, my dear fellow?"

"What is '*pourquoi*'?" Sir Andrew frowns. "Do, or not do?" He sighs wistfully. "I wish I had spent more time on my French. I was all for the fencing and dancing, and of course I couldn't get enough of the bearbaiting. O, had I but followed the arts!" he says with a regretful groan, staring off into space.

"Then you would have had a better head of hair," Sir Toby suggests.

"Would that have mended my hair?"

"Absolutely, for you know it won't curl on its own."

Sir Andrew wonders at the connection. "But it suits me well enough, does it not?"

"Excellently well," Sir Toby assures him. "*It hangs like yarn on the very spindle,*" he says in an affected voice, as though reciting a line of poetry. He comes up beside Sir Andrew. "I hope before too long to see a wife take you between her legs and spin it for all she's worth!" he teases, and pokes Sir Andrew playfully between the legs.

A prude, Sir Andrew steps back, embarrassed. "Well, I'll head home tomorrow, as I said. Your niece will not be seen, or if she will, it's four to one she'll have nothing to do with the likes of me." He puts on a gloomy and defeated look. "The Count who lives close by, he woos her too."

"She'll have nothing to do with the Count," Sir Toby dismisses the idea. "She'll not marry above her station, either for wealth, position or brains. I have heard her swear it. No, there's hope for you yet, man," Sir Toby says with enthusiasm.

"Do you think so?"

"I think nothing else, sir."

Andrew reflects. "Then I suppose I could stay another month…" Suddenly amused, he chuckles to himself. "I must have one of the strangest minds in the world. Sometimes it wanders and all I can think of is dances and merrymaking."

"And you are good at such frivolities, are you not?"

"As good as any man in Illyria," Sir Andrew says, "whoever he is. Except if there are some better," he adds with another chuckle.

All enthusiasm, Sir Toby puts out an arm and slaps him on the back. "How good is your jig, Sir Knight?"

"I can caper like a deer."

"I'm sure you can," Sir Toby snickers wryly, slightly drunk now, while Sir Andrew puts down his wine, raises his arms over his head in a dramatic pose and leaps awkwardly through the air: his clumsiness suggesting he's a terrible dancer.

"As for the backward steps, I'm as good as any man in Illyria—" And before Sir Toby can tell him he'll take him at his word, Sir Andrew throws himself backwards into the air, tripping over his own feet so that when he lands he sails headlong into the wall, below the gold-framed painting of young Olivia and her brother, which crashes down, cracking him on the head.

He gazes sheepishly up at Sir Toby who comes over and helps him back on his feet.

"Why do you hide such things?" demands Sir Toby. "Why would you keep these talents out of sight—curtained off? Will they not grow dusty like your old antiques? If I were you, I would not walk places, but jig. I would even dance my way to the bathroom. So what are you waiting for, sir? Is this a world to hide talents in? I would think, judging by the excellent shape of your legs, you were born to dance."

Encouraged by Sir Toby's apparent confidence, Sir Andrew peers down at his long legs. "They are strong, it's true. And they do look good in bright-colored stockings. Shall we try some dances together?"

"What else should we do? Were we not born under the sign of Taurus?"

"Taurus?" Sir Andrew frowns. "Isn't that for neck and heart?"

"No, it's for legs and thighs," Sir Toby insists. "Let me see you leap again."

His spirits buoyed, Sir Andrew dances happily forth into the hall, Sir Toby lingering behind to retrieve his friend's money pouch, which is lying on the floor near the fallen picture.

"Higher," he calls to Sir Andrew, slipping the pouch in his pocket as he heads out the door. "—Higher, that's it! Ha-ha!"

Dressed as a young man now, her hair tied neatly behind her head in a ponytail, Viola is sitting with Orsino's messenger Valentine in the Duke's palace garden: a series of terraces, each filled with an array of exotic colored flowers and sculptured shrubs and short, oriental trees. Self-conscious and slightly nervous, Viola watches Valentine's motions as much as she listens to what he is saying. Now and again she copies his gestures, assumes a similar posture, or mimics the expressions on his face, Valentine much too absorbed in what he's talking about to notice.

"…In fact, if the Duke continues to hold you in such favor, Cesario, it won't be long until you're promoted. He's known you but three days, and already he has taken you deep into his confidence."

"You sound doubtful, sir, either fearing he will change his mind about me, or that I will not have it within me to carry out the duties with which he has entrusted me. Is he known for being fickle in the way he bestows favors?"

"I have not known him to be."

"I thank you then, sir—but here comes the Duke now."

Flanked by Curio and six or seven gentlemen companions, all of them well-dressed but serious and unsmiling, Orsino comes down the stone stairs to the lowest level of the garden, which affords both a view of the harbor town below and the blue vista of open sea beyond the bay, where several tall ships are passing, their sails puffed to the full in a following wind.

"Has anyone seen Cesario?" the Duke inquires of his friends.

"There, my lord," a gentleman says, and points to the bench where Viola and Valentine are sitting.

"Give us a few moments," the Duke says then turns and hurries over, Valentine bowing as he makes his way along the path to wait with Curio and the others.

"Cesario," Orsino smiles and comes to stand with Viola.

"At your service, my lord," she says and bows, Orsino noticing something pleasantly different about her movements, something more genuine and unpracticed than he is used to.

"Cesario," he starts right in, "you know everything about me. My innermost thoughts, my secret feelings—they're an open book to you. Therefore, be a good friend and say you will return to her for me." Viola begins to speak but he puts up his hand to indicate silence. "Say you won't be denied entry, stand at her door and tell the servants you will stay rooted to the spot until you are permitted to speak with her."

"Surely, my noble lord, if she is as deep in mourning as people say she will not consent to see me."

"Be persistent in your entreaties then, forego politeness if you must, just so long as you gain a hearing for me."

"Say I do, my lord, what then?"

"Why, acquaint her with the intensity of my passions and my love. Impress her with vivid accounts in proof of my utmost devotion. It's much the better that you be the one to represent the sorry state that I am in because of her indifference—she will better accept it coming from someone closer to her age than from an older and less ardent messenger."

"I don't think so, my lord."

"Dear fellow, listen to me: she will." Orsino takes her hands in his and looks pleadingly into her eyes. "For those who would call you a man do disservice to your youthfulness." He studies the rest of her face. "The lips of goddess Diana are not as smooth or more appealing in their cherry redness as yours. Your sweet voice is almost like a girl's, gentle and fetching—in many ways you could but pass for a woman. No one is more perfect for this business on my behalf than you. Please?"

She looks away from him and nods. "I will then."

Still holding her hands, he turns and calls to the others. "Four or five of you go with him—all of you, if you like. I am more content when left alone these days," he says to Viola and lets go of her hands.

"If you succeed in this endeavor, Cesario, you shall live like your lord, as if his fortune were your very own."

"I'll do my best to woo this lady," Viola says and bows, Orsino's companions waiting for her to come over and precede them up the stairs. "—Yet I fear there are problems, and not a few," she says under her breath, "for *I* would rather become his wife, than her he sends me to woo..."

Alone in his garden, the Duke stares out to sea before letting his gaze fall on the harbor town below, and a particular house that stands in Merchant's Row....

The folds of her dress in hand, Maria hurries up the spiral staircase behind a nimble-legged little man in a harlequin outfit named Feste, who has been the family jester since before Olivia was born.

"...No," she calls ahead. "Either tell me where you've been, or I'll not open my lips a crack to make excuses for you. My lady will have you *hung* for being absent."

The bells on the tips of his fool's cap jingling as he comes up the stairs, Feste reaches the second floor landing and moves quickly along the wide, wood-paneled hall. "Let her have me hung," he replies, not caring. "He that is well hung in this world has nothing to fear."

"You'll be hanged for being absent so long, or perhaps dismissed.

Isn't that as good as a hanging to you?

"Many a good hanging prevents a bad marriage," he winks at her. "As for being dismissed, winter isn't far away. I could use the hibernation."

"So you won't tell me where you've been?" she pants as she runs forward and draws even with him.

"'Twill be more fun to keep you *hanging*," he quips.

"Enough of that, you rogue!" she scolds and bats him on the arm as he comes to a stop at a set of double doors. He pretends to be bowled over by her blow then straightens up and begins making last-minute adjustments to his costume, whistling merrily as though no one else is there. "You'd best come up with a clever excuse then!" Maria warns over the sound of his whistling. Feste turns, puts a hand to his lips and blows her a mocking kiss. Hands on her hips, she shakes her head and glares at him, but when he continues to ignore her, she gives up and starts back toward the stairs.

Alone in front of the doors, Feste lets out a long breath. "Wit, if it be your will," he says to himself, "let my fooling prompt them to laughter." He rolls his head from side to side, loosening up. "Those clever people who think they possess you prove often they are nothing but fools." He opens and closes his mouth a few times, clears his throat. "Would that I—who *know* I lack the gift of thee—may pass for a wise man. For as Quinapulus said, 'Better a witty fool than a foolish wit.'"

Ready, he reaches for the handles, throws open the double doors and steps inside the room, calling "God bless you, lady!" as he goes…

Holding his hands sideways to cover his face, the fingers of the top hand splayed in a V so only his mischievous eyes are visible, Feste advances through the large, lavishly furnished room toward a long, polished-wood table near the heavily draped windows where Olivia is going over the household accounts with her steward Malvolio, a thin, severe-looking man dressed in a collarless white shirt and Puritan-black jacket, breeches and stockings.

"Take the fool away," Olivia instructs without looking up, although Malvolio does, turning up his nose at the intruder whom he clearly detests. He barks an order at two servants who are cleaning the fireplace. They put down their brooms and go after Feste, but he leads them a merry chase around the room: whistling, shrieking and taunting them as he turns over chairs behind him, hides behind the drapes then crawls out down below when the servants think they have him—hops wildly over the leather couches, tumbles in a somersault across the floor, gets up and runs behind Malvolio and Olivia, daring the servants to catch him if they can.

"—Didn't you hear, gentlemen? Take the lady away—!" he cries.

"Enough!" screams Olivia and shoots to her feet. "You dried up old fool! I'll put up with your nonsense no longer, you wayward and unruly man!"

Feste dives back over the table, does an acrobatic landing and sits down, his legs and arms crossed. "Two faults, my lady, that can be mended with drink and good advice. For if you give the dried up fool drink, then he's no longer dry. Tell the unruly man to mend his ways, if he does, then he's no longer unruly. If he cannot so mend himself, let the tailor do it, and that way what's mended is nicely patched." The servants rush up and lay their hands on him. "—Virtue that goes bad is only patched with sin, remember—sin that mends its ways is merely patched with virtue." He refuses to uncross his legs and stand up, so the servants have to pick him up by his crossed arms and carry him out. "—If this simple logic convinces you," he calls back to Olivia, "so be it. If it does not, what else can I say—but this loyalty to your dead brother cannot last!" he hollers, "any more than youth can halt its passing!" The servants are about to take him out the door when he squirms hard and wriggles free. "The lady ordered you to take away the fool," he taunts and dashes back to the table. "Therefore I say again," and he points an accusing finger at Olivia, "—take her away!"

"Sir, I ordered them to take *you* away."

"A misjudgment of the highest order, lady—" The servants grab him from behind and hold him but he offers no resistance. "A crown does not a monarch make, my lady, nor cap and bells a fool. Give me leave and I will prove you are a fool."

"You think you can?" she raises an eyebrow.

"Dexteriously, good lady," he deliberately mispronounces.

"Proceed then." Olivia motions for her servants to let him go and takes her seat, Malvolio simmering in resentment at her side.

"But I must question you to do it," Feste says. "Will you be good enough to answer?"

Olivia shrugs. "For want of other pastimes at the moment, I shall."

"First, good lady, tell me why you are in mourning."

"Good fool, for my brother's death."

"But I think his soul is in hell, good lady."

"I know he is in heaven, fool!"

"The more you are the fool then, to mourn for your brother if he is in heaven." He points to her again. "Take the fool away, gentlemen!" Amused, Olivia turns to her steward. "What think you of this fool now? Has he not improved of late?"

"Yes," sneers Malvolio, fixing Feste with a cold glare, "—and will continue to until his death delivers us all from such foolishness. The feebleness of old age, which makes wise men less wise, only makes *fools* more foolish."

"God send you early old-age then, sir," Feste counters with a taunting smile, "—the sooner to increase your foolishness." He puts a hand in front of his face and whispers behind it. "—Sir Toby will swear that I am no conniver before he would wager two cents that you are no fool." He winks and sticks out his tongue

Enjoying herself, Olivia looks to her steward. "What say you to that, Malvolio?"

"Only that I'm amazed your ladyship takes delight in such idle nonsense. The other day I saw him skewered by a street lackey with no more sense than the stones on which he was standing. Just look at him," he regards Feste with disdain, "he has nothing unless you prompt him—I take any who laugh uproariously at these pat fools as no better than the fools themselves."

"I think too high an estimate of your own opinions has soured you against those of others," Olivia says in defense of Feste. "To be sociable, respected and admired means to take things more easily in your stride. We can't take seriously the ridicule of an appointed fool, any more than we can the ravings of the prudish man who rails against what he perceives as our vices."

"Mercury, the god of jesters, bless you, my lady," Feste smiles, taken aback at her chastising of Malvolio.

Maria enters the room and hastens to the table where Olivia is sitting. "There is a young gentleman at the gate who very much desires to speak with you, my lady."

"Is he from Count Orsino?"

"I know not, madam. He's most handsome and is accompanied by a number of attendants."

"Which of my people are waiting with him?"

"Your uncle Sir Toby, madam."

"Goodness no," Olivia exclaims. "Get him away before he shames us all.

"Yes, my lady." Maria bows and leaves. Olivia stands up from the table. "You go, Malvolio. If it be yet another proposal from the count, say I am unwell, or not at home, or whatever you like, just so long as he's got rid of."

Malvolio nods smartly and goes.

Olivia turns a reproachful look on Feste. "Now you see how your fooling grows tedious and uninteresting, fool?"

"But you spoke up for jesters a moment ago, my lady," a disappointed Feste reminds her, "—as if perhaps you had a son who was one of us—" He breaks off when he sees Sir Toby Belch lumbering into the room, short of breath and swaying precariously on his feet as he walks.

"My word, he's half drunk!" declares Olivia, watching her uncle weave his way toward her. "Who is this man at the gate, uncle?"

"A gentleman," Sir Toby answers, his speech noticeably slurred.

"A gentleman? What gentleman?"

"There's a gentleman here," he points back over his shoulder, teetering as though he's about to fall—except Feste comes over quickly and keeps him on his feet. He belches crudely. "Blast these pickled herrings... Fool!" he calls when he realizes whom it is he's leaning on. "—Greetings fool!"

"Good Sir Toby."

"Uncle, uncle," Olivia scolds him. "How have you managed to fall into such drunken lethargy so early in the day?"

"Lechery? I defy lechery!" He squints, trying to focus on her face. "There's someone at the gate."

"So you say, but who is he?"

"Let him be the devil for all I care. Just give me faith, I say." He hiccups. "Well, it doesn't matter anyway," he babbles, "doesn't matter any…" Turning slowly, he ambles out of the room, waving his arms in the air and humming to himself.

"He is still on his feet, my lady," says Feste. "I shall do my best to keep him that way." He bows quickly and makes his way after the departing Sir Toby, who starts up with a drinking song as he enters the hall.

Olivia steps away from the table and out of habit fingers the ruby ring on her right hand as she awaits word on her gentleman visitor.

In a matter of moments, Malvolio breezes importantly back into the room. "Madam, the young fellow swears he will not budge until he has spoken with you. I told him you were sick. He claims he knows this, and says that is precisely why he has come to see you. I told him you were asleep. He seems to have come on that matter as well. What should I tell him, my lady? It seems he has an answer for every excuse."

"Tell him he shall not speak with me, that's all."

"He's been told so, but he says he'll stand at your door like a fence post until you speak with him."

"What kind of man is he?" she asks.

"Why, like any other man."

"No, I mean what manner of man," she says impatiently.

"A most ill-mannered one, my lady. He says he'll speak with you whether you want him to or not."

"What does he look like—how old is he? Tell me that."

"Neither old enough to be a man nor young enough to be a boy. I'd say he's somewhere in between. He *is* very handsome to look at, I will say that, though his voice is noticeably high, if not shrill, when he speaks."

Wondering if there could be something more to this, she stares thoughtfully ahead, once again fingering her ruby ring. "Let him come in then," she finally decides, "—and call my maid."

Malvolio moves quickly to fetch Maria—but she has been listening outside the door and passes him on his way out.

"Bring me my veil," says Olivia, moving to different positions around the room where she can receive the Duke's messenger. Unable to decide, Maria plants her in position and places the black veil over her head, Olivia's features all but invisible under the dark fabric. Maria straightens the folds of Olivia's dress then takes up a position beside her, not a moment before Viola steps into the room, handsome and beautiful at the same time in her jacket and pants of light blue satin, her silver-buckled black shoes.

"The honorable lady of the house, which is she?"

"I will answer for her," says Olivia. "You may speak with me. What is it you want?"

Viola comes the rest of the way forward and bends over in a deep bow. "Most radiant, exquisite and incomparable beauty—" She breaks off and looks to Maria. "Please tell me this is the lady of the house, for I've never seen her. I would rather not waste my words. For besides having worked on their writing, I have taken the trouble to learn them by heart." Olivia can be heard stifling a giggle beneath the veil, which prompts Maria to do the same. "Gentle ladies," Viola appeals to them, "please don't mock me. Mine is a sensitive nature, even to bad manners."

"Where are you from sir?"

"I can say only what I have prepared. An answer to that question would divert me from my speech. Good gentlewoman," she pleads, "give me some assurance that you are indeed the lady of the house, so I may tell you on what business I have come."

"Are you an actor?"

"No," Viola hesitates, "in all honesty I am not. Though despite malicious rumors regarding my heritage, I can tell you I am not what I would seem to be. Are you the lady of the house?"

"Unless I mistake myself, I am."

"If you are she, you are mistaken by not letting on. For what is yours to give may not be yours to withhold. But this goes beyond my instructions. I will proceed with my speech in praise of you, and then elaborate the point of my message."

"Go straight to that point now, if you would. I excuse you from the words of praise."

"Alas, it was with much effort I learned them, and they're very poetic," Viola persists.

"The more likely they are to be false then. Therefore keep them to yourself, sir. I heard you were insolent at my gates and permitted you to come in more to satisfy my curiosity than to hear what you had to say. If you're some mad fool seeking charity, go away. If you're someone perhaps more sane, be brief. The moon is not in that phase where I can tolerate let alone enjoy frivolous talk." She turns away, indicating that the interview is over.

"Will you hoist sail, sir?" Maria suggests and takes Viola by the elbow. "I will show you the way out."

"—No, good sailor," Viola pulls away. "I would stay in port a while longer. "Sweet lady," she appeals to Olivia, "turn me not away…"

"Very well, say what you've come to say."

"I am a messenger—"

"Surely you have some terrible news to impart if the introduction is this unwieldy. State your business and be done with it."

"It is only for your ears. And I bring no declaration of war, no demand for payment of a debt. I come bearing the olive branch—my words as peaceful as they are important."

"Yet you began by being rude. Who are you? What *is* it you want?" Olivia demands.

"Any rudeness on my part was prompted by the way I was treated when I arrived," Viola explains. "As for who I am and what I want, these are secrets of an intimate kind—sacred to your ears, blasphemy to all others." With her eyes she indicates Maria.

Olivia turns to her maid. "Leave us. I will hear these *holy* words."

Maria hesitates, but receiving a nod from Olivia, turns for the door and leaves.

"Now, sir, you may deliver your *sacred* text."

Viola composes herself then begins. "Most sweet lady—"

"Flattering words," Olivia interrupts, "with much to be said for them, but what do they concern?"

"Orsino's heart."

"His heart? What chapter of his heart?"

"To answer by the book, the first chapter."

"Ah, but you see I've read it, sir. And none of it is true. Have you nothing else to say?"

"Good lady, let me see your face."

"Have you been instructed by your lord to negotiate with my face? You've wandered from your so-called *text*, it seems to me. But we will draw the curtain and show you the picture nonetheless." She lifts her veil. "Look, sir: this is the most recent portrait of me. Is it not well done?" The sarcasm in her voice is mocking rather than bitter.

Viola is taken aback at the beauty of Olivia's face. "—Beauteously done, as if God was its artist," she exclaims.

"The features have been etched to withstand wind and weather."

"It is loveliness and grace married together…the hue of your eyes, your perfect skin and blushing lips painted by nature's sweet and artful hand." A look of worry crosses her face. "But my lady, you are the cruellest woman alive if you take all this beauty to the grave and leave the world no copy."

"Sir, you need not fear," Olivia continues in her mock-serious tone. "I will not be so hard-hearted. I will publish diverse catalogues of my beauty. It shall be detailed, every element and item labeled as I choose. For instance, Item: two gray eyes, with lids attached. Item: one neck, accompanying chin, and so forth. —But surely you weren't sent here to appraise me?"

"I see what you are: you are too proud. Though even if you were the devil, you are beautiful. My lord and master loves you," she pleads, "with a love whose only reward would be to see you crowned the very paragon of beauty."

"How does he love me?"

"In worshipping adoration, with prayerful tears and longing sighs."

"Your lord knows my decision," Olivia says dismissively. "I cannot love him, yet I am assured he is a good man, by wealth and nobility possessed, a most valiant, intelligent and capable man, gracious in every regard, handsome in every particular. But I simply cannot love him, sir. He should have accepted that long ago."

"If I loved you as longingly as my master does," Viola protests, "and with such suffering anguish, your refusal to return my love would seem incomprehensible. I would not understand it—"

"—But what could you do?"

"I could build myself a cabin of willow boughs at your gate," Viola blurts, "and cry out to you within your house. I could write moving *chansons* of unrequited love and sing them even in the dead of night. I could shout your name to the resounding hills so the echoes would cry 'Olivia! Olivia!' You would never again find rest in this world unless you took pity on me."

Their eyes meet in the silence that follows, Olivia—clearly agitated by something that has been stirred up inside her—the first to look away. "You will achieve much," she says, resuming her cool and aloof manner. "What is your lineage, your family background?"

"More distinguished than it presently appears. My social standing is worthy of regard. I am a gentleman."

Olivia considers for a moment. "Go back to your lord," she says. "I cannot love him. Let him send no more emissaries to me either—unless, perhaps, you come again…to tell me how he takes my decision." She meets Viola's stare, but grows uneasy and immediately looks away. "In the meantime," she says stiffly, "I thank you for your trouble and bid you farewell." She produces a small purse, takes out a coin and offers it to Viola. "Have this for your efforts."

Viola sneers in resentment. "I am no messenger to be tipped," she protests. "Keep your money! It is my master, not me, who deserves payment. May love make the heart of him you love as cold as ice one day, your passion—like my master's now—treated with contempt. Farewell, cruel beauty."

Without bowing, she turns and makes for the door. Alone in the room, Olivia fingers her ruby ring and murmurs to herself. "'What is your rank?' 'Above my present station, but my social standing is worthy of regard. I am a gentleman.'" She smiles. "You are indeed. Your voice, your face, your gestures, manners and conduct are those of a well-bred man. But not so fast. Get hold of yourself…" She paces near the curtained windows, flustered and confused. "If only the master were this man. Now, now," she cautions herself, "may one catch the fever so quickly? So quickly sense this young man's perfections working their delicate and invisible power on my affections? Well, so be it. Malvolio!" she calls to her steward.

He sails into the room a moment later and rushes to her side.

"Run after that rude messenger who was just here, the count's servant." She hands him her ruby ring. "He pressed this upon me against my will. Tell him I refuse to accept it—and request that he encourage his lord not to expect my favor at any time in the future. I am not the woman for him. If the young man will return tomorrow, I will give him reasons why."

"I will, madam," Malvolio replies, a gloating smile crossing his face as he hurries off.

Olivia touches her hands to her face, feeling the flush that has come into her cheeks. "I know not what I've started here. That my eyes play tricks on my mind, I fear. Fate let me feel your guiding hand, that what will be, will be, according to your plan...."

Picking up her veil from the floor where it has fallen, she walks slowly to the double doors, pausing part way to look down at her hands. A smile forming on her lips, she throws down the veil and, still smiling, continues for the door....

A hand holding his tall-crowned black hat on his head, Malvolio dashes down the street past the great mansions along Merchant's Row, so intent on catching up to Viola and the Duke's departing attendants that he isn't watching where he's going: his feet splash in a sizeable puddle left over from the storm a few days earlier. He shrieks in dismay and glances down at his dripping-wet stockings and waterlogged shoes, but he can't stop now—Viola and her attendants are about to go round a storm-felled tree that has yet to be cleared away from the road, beyond which the Duke's coach is waiting to leave.

"You there!" Malvolio calls in a panic. "Young man!"

Viola and the attendants stop walking and turn, amused to see the notoriously pompous Malvolio in such discomposure. His shoes weighed down by water, he hobbles more than walks up to them and indicates that it is Viola with whom he has business. The attendants carry on toward the coach, offering snickered comments loud enough for Malvolio to hear, although he puts on a haughty air and pretends not to.

"The Countess is returning this to you, sir." Malvolio produces Olivia's ruby red ring and holds it up. "You might have saved me the trouble if you had just taken it with you when you left," he sneers. "—She wishes me to add as well, that you make clear to your lord she will have nothing more to do with him. And one thing more: you should not be so bold as to come again on his behalf, unless it be to report on how your lord has taken the ring being sent back. Take it, go ahead."

"She accepted the ring from me," Viola says innocently. "I'll not take it back."

"Come, sir. You rudely threw it at her, and she desires that it should be returned the same way." He throws the ring in Viola's face; it bounces off her and falls to the ground. "If it be worth stooping for, there it lies, if not for you, then for anyone who finds it." His duty done, he throws his chin in the air with disdain, turns about and heads back up the street, the wet stockings squishing inside his shoes as he walks.

Viola bends down and retrieves the ruby ring. "I left no ring with her—what does she mean by giving it to me like this?" She reflects for a moment. "Heaven forbid that she was enamored with my looks," the thought dawns on her. "She did look at me closely, indeed very close, so that my appearance seemed to register with her. She spoke in a halting way afterwards. That must be it, she's fallen in love." She smiles at her next thought. "The cunning woman. Sending her surly messenger to invite me back so she can see me again…"

The attendants call to her from the coach. She waves that she's heard and is on her way. "Of course she won't accept Orsino's ring: he never sent her one. *I* am the man she desires. If this is so—and it seems to be—poor lady, she might as well love a ghost." She looks down at her clothes as she starts to walk. "Disguise, I see what you have wickedly done in your cunning fashion. How easy it is for the false but handsome man to make an impression in the hearts of women wanting love. Methinks our weakness is the cause, not our nature. But what we are, we are made to be.

She passes around the tree, reflecting on what's happened. "My master loves her dearly, while I, like a fool, have grown as fond of him, and here this countess, quite by mistake, now dotes on me. What can become of this? As long as I am a man, I have no hope of winning the love of my master, yet as a woman—which I do regret—what pangs of longing shall poor Olivia feel? O time you must untangle this, not I," she says to herself as she reaches the coach. "It is too hard a knot for me to untie…" The footman helps her up the bottom step and she gets in. Up front, the driver clicks his reins and Orsino's splendid coach moves off….

The moon is up and shining bright on a desolate stretch of the Illyrian coast, waves crashing on the jagged rocks along the shore as two shadowy figures emerge from a cloud of flying spray and scramble toward an open piece of ground up above where the pounding surf can't reach them. Both wearing bandanas and swords, they bend over and rest their hands on their knees until they catch their breath.

"Why will you not have me go with you?" asks the bigger of the two men, a gold ring in each of his ears.

"Thanks, Antonio, but no," the other replies. "I would not have you risk your own fortunes on one whose future is so uncertain and foreboding. Let me face my hardships alone. To have you suffer more on my behalf is hardly the way to repay you for all you've done."

"Tell me where you're headed at least, sir," says Antonio.

"No, it's better you didn't know," the other man tells him. Besides, I have no clear plan, other than in my grief to wander the land around."

Both men are silent for a moment in the moonlight, waves continuing to break on the rocks below.

"Although I'm not one to pry, sir," Antonio offers, "I can see there is some secret you would keep from me. If you have need to free your mind of troubling thoughts, well, I have always been a good listener, sir…"

The other man gazes at the ocean. "In truth there is, Antonio. Though you know me as Roderigo, my name is Sebastian. My late father was governor of Messalina, you might have heard his name. He died several years ago, leaving behind two children, my sister and I, who were born but a few minutes apart. I wish the heavens had seen fit to have us die together as well. But you prevented that by rescuing me, sir, for about an hour before you pulled me from the pounding surf, I saw her go down with our ship."

"A sad day. I am sorry, sir"

"People said the resemblance between us was great, although in my eyes and for many others, she was the beauty. I will tell you this much: she had a mind which even our worst enemies admired." His voice shaking as he speaks, tears well up in his eyes. "And now…" he fights back tears, "she is drowned in the salt sea waters—and now I am about to drown her memory in my own." He wipes a hand across his eyes.

"Forgive me, sir," says Antonio, "that I wasn't there to save her."

"No, Antonio," Sebastian responds, "it is *I* who must ask forgiveness, for what I've put you through."

"Perhaps, rather than part ways, I could be your servant, sir."

"You are an adventurer, Antonio. To stay here with me would be undoing all you've done—I've kept you from your voyage long enough. I am bound for the court of Count Orsino. Farewell." After embracing Antonio, he turns and heads toward a thick stand of trees. Finding a path, he soon disappears in the forest darkness...

"The blessing of the gods go with you," Antonio murmurs then gazes out to sea. "I have many enemies at Orsino's court, otherwise I would join you there." After a few moments, he glances at the woods where Sebastian has gone. Tightening the bandana on his head, he adjusts the sword-belt at his waist. "Come what may," he decides, and starts for the forest, "I find myself admiring thee so, that danger is but sport to me—to Duke Orsino's I will go...."

It's after midnight in Olivia's parlor and the candles are burning low, a boisterously drunk Sir Toby, tankard in hand, jabbing an iron poker at the log smoldering in the fireplace, growling at it to start burning. Behind him, Sir Andrew Aguecheek sits slumped in an armchair, drunk and feeling sorry for himself.

"Perk up, Sir Andrew. Perk up, sir." Sir Toby sets down the poker and comes over. "Not to be in bed after midnight is really to be up early. You know the old saying—he thinks a moment before mumbling in made-up Latin—*"Dilu-culo sur-gary."*

"No, indeed I don't know it," Sir Andrew yawns. "But I *do* know that to be up late is to be up late."

"A bad conclusion, sir. As bad as an empty tankard." He hoists his and drinks, a worried frown on his face when he notices it's getting empty. He pulls up a footstool and sits himself down in front of Sir Andrew. "If you're up after midnight, and go to bed then, why it's early morning. So to go to bed after midnight, is to go to bed early. Are these not the four elements of which our life consists: earth, air, fire and water?"

"I suppose," Sir Andrew pouts. "Though in your case I would say they consist of eating and drinking."

"Exactly, sir!" Toby says, slapping Sir Andrew on the knee as he stands up. "I knew you were a scholar. Here's to eating and drinking— Maria!" he shouts, "a jug of wine for my scholarly friend!"

But when the door opens a moment later it is Feste who enters the room, still in his jester's clothes and belled cap, deftly juggling three eggs in the air.

"How now, my worthies!" he calls, breaking his rhythm to let one egg drop so it almost hits the floor in front of Sir Andrew—before he grabs it and tosses it back into the air.

"Welcome, rascal!" Sir Toby grins and swigs from his tankard.

"Hello, fool," Sir Andrew mopes, less than amused by Feste's antics.

"Sir Longface," Feste teases, pitching the eggs so they land in Sir Andrew's lap…without breaking: they're hard-boiled, which finally puts a smile on Sir Andrew's face.

"Give us a song, fool!" Sir Toby urges.

Feste puts on a mock-serious frown, touches a finger to his temple and thinks.

"The fool has an excellent voice," Sir Andrew mumbles wistfully. "I would pay money for a voice like his." He looks at the eggs in his lap. Taking one in each hand, he puzzles over what to do with the third. "You were certainly funny last night," he compliments Feste, "when you spoke of 'Pigro-gromitus and the Vapians passing the equinoctial of Que-ubus.'" He chuckles and shakes his head. "It was very good, indeed—I sent you sixpence for your sweetheart, did you get it?"

Feste bows to Sir Andrew and takes back the eggs. "I impetticoated your graciosity indeed, sir, for Malvolio sticks his nose in everything." He puts up the hand holding the eggs and whispers behind it, "Psst! My lady has expensive tastes, sir, and beer is not cheap at The Myrmidons Tavern." He gives a lewd wink then holds up the eggs for Sir Andrew to see, and in a single move stuffs them in his mouth, but when he pulls his hands away the next moment, his mouth is empty, and the eggs have disappeared.

"Excellent!" cries Sir Andrew, sitting up in his chair. "Why, this is the best fool there ever could be. Let's have a song after all!"

Feste cocks an eyebrow at Sir Toby.

"All right, there's sixpence for you," the big man complains, but takes out a coin and hands it over.

"There's sixpence from me too," Sir Andrew says, copying Sir Toby. "If one man gives, and another—" he begins a joke, but Feste interrupts.

"—Would you have a love song or a song to good life?"

"A love song," Sir Toby roars, "a love song!"

"Yes," Sir Andrew agrees. "I'm not one for the good life…" He returns to his chair and waits for the song, a gleeful grin on his face.

Feste puts on a hurt face and begins. *Oh mistress mine, where do you roam? When will it be, that you come home? I yearn for you by night, by day. Absence makes no heart grow fonder, makes not lovers' love grow stronger, as the foolish wise men say. Come back to me, my pretty sweet thing—your journey end with our lips meeting.*

"Well done indeed!" Sir Andrew exclaims.

"Very good, fool," Sir Toby adds, Feste holding up a finger to quiet them so he can continue.

"What is love? We'll find it not hereafter: present joys bring present laughter. What's to come remains unsure; waiting means my arms stay empty. Come and kiss me, sweet and twenty—youth's a time will not endure."

"A mellifluent voice, as I'm a true knight," Sir Andrew applauds, rising from his chair.

"A fetching voice," Sir Toby chimes in.

"Very sweet and fetching," says Sir Andrew.

"If we heard with our noses," Sir Toby allows, "it would have a fetching aroma too!" Suddenly rambunctious, he slaps Sir Andrew on the back. "Shall we wake the night owl with something fetching ourselves? Should we do that?"

"We should!" Sir Andrew replies. "We must! I'm a *dog* for something fetching!"

"Indeed, sir," the fool teases, "and some dogs fetch well."

"That they do!" Sir Andrew agrees, the pun going over his head.

"Let our fetch be," he puts a finger to his lips while he thinks, then claps his hands. "—I know. Let it be *'You knave, you knight'*"

"*'Hold your peace, you knave, you knight'*?"

"*'Hold your peace,'*" Sir Andrew nods.

"But I'll have to call you a knave, knight," Feste warns.

"It won't be the first time I've forced someone to call me a knave," Sir Andrew says defiantly, missing Feste's humor again. "You start it off, fool," he says but begins singing himself. *"Hold your peace, you knave, you knight—"*

"How do I start it off if I'm holding my peace?" Feste demands.

"True, fool!" Sir Andrew laughs. "How can you begin when—"

"Hold your peace," Sir Toby cuts in then lifts his tankard and drains it.

Feste sounds the opening note. Sir Toby hums the next interval, Sir Andrew the harmony above that. They hold their parts until Feste is satisfied and waves his hand for them to stop.

"Hold your peace, you knave, you knight…" he commences.

"Hold your peace, you knave, you knight," Sir Toby joins in, his voice booming.

Mouthing the words to himself, Sir Andrew bobs his head in time to their singing, but just when it's time for his turn—Maria storms into the room and confronts them, hands planted firmly on her hips.

"What is going *on* that you must make this unearthly racket!" she screams over the sound of the singing, which abruptly stops. Red-faced and angry, she fixes them with a livid glare. "The devil knows why my lady hasn't called her steward and ordered him to throw you out!"

Sir Toby rears up in a defensive posture. "Never mind your threats, my lady, we are wise to them. Malvolio's a fool and a prig, while," he sings: *"Three merry men be we!* Am I not a relative?" he demands. "Am I not her own flesh and blood? Nonsense, lady!" He sings again: *"Dwelt a man in old Camptown, doo-dah, doo-dah!"*

Furious, Maria fixes him with a disgusted scowl and shakes her head.

Holding his sides, Feste gives a high-pitched laugh. "Curse me, but the knight's a raving good fool!"

"That he is," Sir Andrew agrees. "He's foolish enough when he's in the mood. And I am too," he adds proudly, "though *he* does it with more style. I, on the other hand, am a natural born fool."

"—*On the twelfth day of Christmas,*" Sir Toby bursts out singing.

"—*My true love gave to me,*" Feste joins in.

"For the love of God, peace!" shrieks Maria above the sound of their raucous singing, however her face is suddenly swept with a look of fear: an irate Malvolio is marching into the room, an amusing sight in his nightgown, sleeping cap and slippers.

"Are you mad, my masters!" he calls out. "What do you *think* you are doing? Do you have no more common sense, manners or *decency* than to wail like demented gypsies at this time of night, turning my lady's house into a tavern by squawking your disgraceful ditties at the tops of your voices! Do you have no respect for persons, place or time?"

"'Ditties'?" Sir Toby laughs hilariously. "Go hang yourself, sir, and your 'ditties' too!"

"Sir Toby, I will be frank with you. My lady bade me inform you that although she gives you a home here in bonds of kinship, she feels no kinship whatsoever when it comes to your loutish and unruly conduct. If you can behave properly, you are welcome to stay; if not, and you would rather live elsewhere, she is more than willing to bid you farewell."

"*Farewell dear heart, since I must needs be gone,*" Sir Toby sings to Maria in mock lament, and reaches out his arms to embrace her.

"No, good Sir Toby—" she protests mildly and backs away.

"*Come now, my sweet,*" Feste improvises with a pleading look on his face, "*his days are almost done.*"

"So that's how it will be then?" Malvolio demands sternly.

"*But I will never die,*" Sir Toby continues serenading Maria.

"*Sir Toby, there you lie,*" says Feste, bowing his head in mourning.

"*Shall I tell him where to go?*" Sir Toby inquires.

"*Of course, sir, you should do so.*"

"*Shall I tell him where to go and care not?*"

"*Oh, no, no, no, you dare not!*"

Sir Toby winces. "You're off key, sir—and yes I dare." He turns on Malvolio. "Are you anything more than a steward, sir? Do you think, because you are so saintly, there will be no more cakes and ale in this house, no more merrymaking, no festivity nor fun?"

"*Farewell, O spice of life...* " Feste sings in mock sorrow.

"—To the spice of life!" Sir Toby hoists his tankard in jubilation, but doesn't drink. "Go, sir," he barks at Malvolio. "Polish up your steward's chain. —A jug of wine, Maria!" He catches Feste's eye, who makes mocking gestures behind Malvolio's back then plucks his nightcap off his head and tosses it to Sir Andrew, who pitches it to Sir Toby, who throws it into the fire.

Fuming, Malvolio fixes Maria with a cold glare. "Mistress Mary, if you value my lady's opinion at anything more than contempt, you would not furnish the drink that fuels this brawling behavior. I can assure you that this will be made known to her. Goodnight!" Turning about, he moves quickly in his slippers toward the door, and departs, Feste scampering out the door right behind.

"O, go fly a kite!" Maria snipes after him.

His eyes narrowed, Sir Andrew has the beginnings of a belligerent look on his face. "It would be like drink to a hungry man to challenge him to a duel," he declares, clenching his teeth, "—and then not show up to fight! *That* would make a fool out of him."

"Do it, knight!" Sir Toby says keenly. "I'll write a challenge for you myself, or deliver your words of indignation to him in person."

"Sweet, Sir Toby," Maria cautions him, "since the Duke's young man visited my lady today, she hasn't been herself. As for Monsieur Malvolio, leave him to me. If I can't make his name the byword for stupidity, and turn him into the laughing-stock of the town, then you can say I haven't enough brains to keep from falling out of bed."

"Tell us what you have in mind," Sir Toby demands, his interest mounting.

"Yes, tell us," Sir Andrew choruses.

"Well, sirs, sometimes he can be such a puritan it's almost unbearable."

"—O, if I thought that, I'd beat him like a dog!" Sir Andrew declares valiantly.

"What, for being a puritan or unbearable? And what clever reason would you have for doing that, dear knight?"

Sir Andrew stares uncertainly. "Perhaps not a clever reason, but I would have a good one, you can be sure…"

"—However," Maria carries on, "he's not always that way. It's more when it suits him, or when others of importance are around. He's a vain, self-serving so-and-so, an affected ass who is always playing up to his betters with his prim words and practiced manners. He has the highest opinion of himself and is so crammed with feelings of his own superiority he firmly believes that all who look upon him love him." She puts on a wicked smile. "And it's of that weakness, sirs, which my revenge will most potently take advantage."

"What will you do?" Sir Toby presses her.

She puts on a mischievous grin. "Leave some anonymous love letters where he'll be sure to discover them. He'll find himself the object of the writer's affection: his face, his clothes, the way he walks, even his manner of speaking. I can write just like your niece my lady," she looks to Sir Toby. "Reading a note we've both forgotten but rediscovered, we can hardly tell by whom it was first written."

"Excellent! I smell a plot!" Sir Toby cries.

"I can smell it too," Sir Andrew adds helpfully.

Sir Toby pieces the scheme together. "—He'll think, from the letters you leave for him to find, that they're from my niece, and so will conclude that she's in love with him."

"My plan is indeed a horse of that color," Maria says.

"And your horse will make an *ass* of him!" Sir Andrew puts in.

Maria smiles at him. "An ass indeed."

"Wonderful, I say!" Sir Andrew rejoices. "Excellent!"

"It will be great sport, I guarantee it," Maria assures him. "I know my medicine will work on him." In high spirits, Sir Toby and Sir Andrew join arms and cavort in celebration until Maria gets their attention. "—Further, I will hide you two, along with Fabian, in the place where he will find the letters, and you can see for yourselves exactly how he receives them. For tonight, we should be off to bed where we can dream about the ass Malvolio is sure to make of himself." She places her hand on Sir Toby's tankard. He puts his hand over hers, and looks to Sir Andrew, who hesitates a moment but finally puts down his hand to seal the pact. Maria nods goodnight and then goes.

"Good night, my little bulldog," Sir Toby offers in praise of her spunk.

"If you ask me, she's as good a wench as you could find," Sir Andrew declares.

"A perfect bulldog," Sir Toby says. "And, she adores me," he boasts. "What do you think of that?"

"I was adored once too…" Sir Andrew says with a melancholy frown.

"Let's go to bed, knight," Sir Toby suggests. "You need to send for more money."

"If I can't win your niece's love, I'll be in a very bad way."

"—Send for more money, knight. If you don't win her in the end you can have me whipped."

"If I don't, never trust me again…take that how you will."

"Come knight, we'll crack some winc. It's too late for bed now."

He takes Sir Andrew by the arm and heads for the door, a satisfied smile spreading across his face at the way things are turning out….

Sunlight streaming in through the windows, Duke Orsino has come to paint in the gallery hall earlier than usual this morning and is already busy at work when the door at the end of the hall bursts open and Curio comes in, pointing Viola to stand alongside the musicians as they take up their positions and prepare to play.

"Good morning, friends," Orsino greets them without looking up from his work. He continues painting for several moments, turning to glance at Curio after he exchanges a smaller brush for a larger one. "Is it possible to hear that ancient melody that was sung for us last night?" He resumes painting. "It brought much relief to my suffering heart— my mood today calls for something more settling and somber than these sprightly dances and popular songs."

"The one who would perform it isn't here, my lord," Curio replies.

"Who is that?"

"Feste the jester, my lord, the fool who greatly delighted the Lady

Olivia's father. It is possible he may still be somewhere about."

"Go find him, if you would, and in the meantime let me have just the tune."

Curio starts the musicians in a slow, lamenting tune then hurries out...

"—Come here, my boy," Orsino calls to Viola, but she doesn't hear because of the music. She stays where she is until he holds up one of his brushes and motions her to approach, waving her to stand just back from the easel so he can see her while he paints.

"If ever you are in love, Cesario, remember me in the sweet discomfort of your passion. For what I am suffering through, all lovers do: restless and distracted, we are given to melancholy in all our thoughts and feelings, except those for the one who is beloved." His words making her uneasy, she averts her eyes. "How do you find this tune?" he asks, switching his larger brush for the smaller one again.

"It truly expresses what the heart can feel," she answers.

He smiles. "You speak as though from experience—upon my life," he breaks into a grin, "young as you are, your eye has spotted a face that it loves, hasn't it?"

"You could say it has, my lord," she offers, looking at him only when his attention turns back to the painting.

"What sort of woman is she?" He concentrates on the painting.

Nervous, Viola clutches her hands in front of her. "Not unlike you, my lord."

"She isn't good enough for you then," he scoffs lightly. "How old is she?"

"About your age, my lord."

He chuckles. "Which is too old. A woman should have someone older than herself so she can more readily win over and firmly hold the affections of his heart. For, my boy, however much we men praise ourselves, our love is apt to be more rash and unsteady, more wavering, more easily won and lost, than women's."

"I'm sure that is so, my lord."

"Be sure your love is younger than you, or your feelings for her won't last. Women are like roses, whose fair beauty once displayed, begins quickly to fade."

"Indeed, they are like roses, but alas that they are so and must die just as to perfection they grow."

Feste following behind him, Curio returns to the hall.

"Ah, good fellow," Orsino calls, motioning Feste over. "Come, let's hear the song we had from you last night. Listen up, Cesario. In olden days the women at their spinning, the carefree maidens weaving and the knitters in the sunshine would sing it while they worked. It offers simple truths and touches sweetly on the innocence of love, as it was in bygone days."

"Shall I begin, sir?" Feste asks.

"By all means. Let us hear it, fool."

Feste nods, then, with all eyes on him, he lets his head hang down as he strolls near the middle of the room, eyes downcast, his expression one of sorrow. "'*Come away, come away, death...and in my coffin let me be laid. Fly away. Fly away, breath...I'm slain by a fair cruel maid. My shroud of white...happily I wear it. My dying heart,*'" he has tears in his eyes, "*no one did ever share it. So no flowers, no flowers sweet, on my black coffin let there be strewn. Not a friend, not a friend shall greet...my poor corpse, where it wastes in ruin. A thousand, thousand sighs to save, lay me down deep, where no true love shall find my grave...and sit down by it...and for me sadly weep.*'" Tears running down his cheeks, he closes his eyes and gravely bows his head to end the song.

Turning from his painting, Orsino waves Feste to approach, noticing Viola has turned her head away. But he thinks nothing of it. "This is for your trouble," he says to Feste as he comes and stands beside the easel.

"No trouble," the fool smiles, the tears gone from his face. "I take pleasure in singing, sir."

"I'll pay for your pleasure then," the Duke says, and hands him some coins.

"Truly, sir," says Feste as he pockets the money, "pleasure must be paid for sooner or later."

"Indeed it must," Orsino agrees and goes back to painting.

"May the god of melancholy protect thee, sir," Feste offers some words of wisdom, "and the tailor make your jackets of many colors to match your ever-changing moods. As for myself, I would have men so apt at changing sent to sea. Then their business could be with everyone, and their destination anywhere, for truly, sir, that makes all the difference between a good voyage, and a bad." He bows dutifully and turns to go, but something about the painting catches his eye and he hesitates for a moment before making his way to the door, meeting Viola's glance as he passes, her eyes red from crying.

"—Cesario," the Duke calls and beckons her forward. She steps up to the easel and bows. "Return once more to this supremely cruel woman. Tell her that my love, the noblest in the world, prizes not vast quantities of land, neither riches plentiful nor scant as fortune has bestowed. Rather it is the dazzling, gem-bright beauty with which nature has adorned her that attracts my soul."

"But if she still cannot love you, sir—"

"I cannot accept such an answer from her."

"But in truth you *must*, my lord," Viola holds her ground. "Suppose there was some other lady, as perhaps there is," she says, "who has as great and strong a love for you as you feel for your Olivia. But you cannot love her, and thus you tell her so. Must she not accept that answer then?"

He shakes his head in protest. "There is no woman's heart that could endure the beating of so great a passion as love gives to mine. No woman's heart is big enough to feel as much at one time. And never forget, sir, that for women, love is no more than a whim, a passing fancy—a matter of taste and not of passion. They tire more readily than we, grow impatient and distracted within a sudden moment if it suits them, but my love is all-consuming as the sea and devours as much. You cannot compare the love a woman could have for me, with that which I feel for Olivia."

"Of course not, my lord, but I know—"

"What do you know?"

"—Too well what love women may have for men. Indeed, they are as faithful as we are," she insists. "My father had a daughter who loved a man, just as, perhaps, if I were a woman, I might love your lordship."

"And what's her story?"

"A blank page, my lord. She never revealed her love but kept it

TWELFTH NIGHT • 44

always hidden. She pined away with thinking about it, and with a pale and downcast face would brood like the figure of Patience atop tombstones, smiling as though accepting of her grief. Was this not a love indeed? We men may say more and declare ourselves more boldly, though much of this, in truth, is oft for show, for in our vows both truth and lies contend: but little do we really love, in the end."

"And did your sister die from love, my boy?"

"I am the only daughter in my father's house—the only child as far as I now know. Shall I go to this lady, sir?"

"Yes, go quickly. And give her this jewel." From the worktable beside him, he takes a small blue case and holds it out to her. "—Say the Count Orsino will not yield, that only by Olivia's love can his wounded heart be healed."

Viola accepts the jewel case and bows, but as she turns away her glance falls on the portrait the Duke is painting, and she starts: the young woman in the picture has a face very like her own....

In contrast to the darkness and gloom inside the house, Olivia's garden is a bright Mediterranean paradise of trimmed hedges, lush plants and colorful exotic flowers: curving crushed-quartz pathways, standing stone sculpture, obelisks and urns interspersed with water-fountains and trickling streams that flow into a circular pond where large goldfish glide quietly just beneath the surface.

Puffing and perspiring as he lumbers along the garden's main path, Sir Toby is wearing an old blue-and-white naval uniform, the gold braid coming loose around the jacket collar, a soiled scarlet sash draped across his great barrel chest. Looking ill at ease without his tankard, he reaches a marble bench seat and, with a sigh of relief, sits down.

"Come along, Master Fabian," he calls to a rustic-looking young man nearby who stamps his foot at several peacocks, their gold, green and blue feathers spread wide to prevent him from getting by. They cry in protest but turn away when he stamps again.

"—I'll come all right," he answers and hurries to join Sir Toby. "If

I miss a moment of this, why they can boil me to death in a pot of my own misery."

"It will be something to see the pompous, meddling fool humiliated, won't it?"

"I will rejoice, Master Toby. You know that he wanted your niece to dismiss me over that bear-baiting business?"

Sir Toby shakes his head. "No matter now. We'll have the bear back again and set it upon *him* this time!" He glances across the garden. "—We'll mock him without mercy, will we not?" he hollers to Sir Andrew Aguecheek, the tall, lean knight keeping an apprehensive eye on the strutting peacocks as he passes them.

"If we don't, life won't be worth living!" Aguecheek replies, approaching Sir Toby who can only shake his head in wonder at the apricot-colored suit of clothes and orange paten-leather shoes his friend is wearing—a long-brimmed orange hat on his head to protect his pale skin from the glare of the noonday sun.

Fabian nudges Sir Toby and points across the garden: Maria is bustling forward in a flurry of excitement, the anonymous letter in her hand.

"Here's our little villain," Sir Toby smiles. "How now, my precious?" he calls.

"Quickly," she says, running up, "behind the hedge, Malvolio's coming. He's been over yonder in the sun practicing fancy bows to his own shadow for the past half hour." She shoos the three of them toward an opening in the hedge. "—Get ready for some laughter," she chuckles and holds up the letter, "for this is sure to make a blustering idiot out of him." She giggles but quickly puts on a straight face. "Keep down, for heaven's sake," she says, and positions Sir Toby to one side of the opening through which they'll watch, "and you there," she has Fabian stand on the other side. She takes in Sir Andrew's gaudy orange outfit and snickers as, much to his dismay, she makes him crouch down and back himself behind the hedge so he's on his knees in front of Sir Toby. "—So, here is the bait." She waves the letter. "—And here comes the fish that will take it…"

In his usual black clothes despite the warm weather, Malvolio is taking his own sweet time as he walks along the garden path, so absorbed in a lively conversation he is having with himself that he doesn't see Maria set the letter down on a standing, burnished brass sundial and rush off through an arbor of pink roses to another part of the garden…

"It's in fortune's hands," sighs Malvolio. "It's all in fortune's hands. Although Maria did tell me once that Olivia was fond of me. And I've even heard my lady say that, were she to fall in love, it would be with someone not unlike me. Besides, she treats me much better than anyone else in her employ. Am I wrong to make something of all this?" he wonders, but answers himself the next moment as a smug smile comes over his face.

"There's one conceited scoundrel!" Sir Toby says under his breath to Fabian and Sir Andrew.

"Hush!" Fabian hisses, and waves Sir Toby not to be so loud. "Lunacy becomes him," he whispers. "Look how he struts about like a peacock—with only the feathers missing!"

"By God," Sir Andrew says bitterly, "I could give him such a beating!

"—Shh!" Sir Toby whispers, and points at Malvolio who is nearing the sundial.

"To be 'Count Malvolio'…"

"The nerve of him!" Sir Toby sneers.

"Shoot him!" Sir Andrew says, and makes a fist. "Shoot him!"

"Quiet!" Fabian tells them.

"—It's not unknown to have happened. Lady Strachy married Dockins, the servant in charge of her wardrobe…"

"Curse him, the witch!"

"Witch?" Fabian winces and makes a face.

"Pipe down both of you," Sir Toby says. "He's more full of himself by the minute. Look how caught up he is—"

"—Having been married to her for, let us say three months, I sit in my stateroom—"

"O for a slingshot to take out his eyes!" Sir Toby cries.

"—I call my household staff around me, dressed in my silk-lined velvet robe, having come from the divan where I left Olivia sleeping—"

"Fire and brimstone!" Sir Toby rails.

"—And then, assuming my most stately manner, and after letting my firm gaze travel solemnly over the faces of my staff—which reminds them that, as I know my place, I expect them to know theirs—I call for my kinsman Toby—"

"Bring me bolts and chains!" Sir Toby snaps, and fights to restrain himself.

"Quiet, quiet, quiet!" Fabian scolds, trying to hear what Malvolio's now saying…

"—Seven of my servants run swiftly off to find him. I frown meanwhile," he does, "perhaps wind my watch," he does so, "or play with some rich jewel I'm wearing," he fingers the gold steward's chain and medallion draped around his neck. "—At which point Sir Toby approaches, and bows in front of me—"

"I could kill him!"

"Stay quiet, Sir Toby!"

"—I extend my hand to him like so," he puts out his hand, "replacing my usual smile with a look of stern authority—"

"And he punches you in the mouth!"

"—Saying, 'Cousin Toby, fortune, having made me husband to your niece, allows me the right to speak to you—"

"What? *What?*" Sir Toby can hardly believe his ears…

"'—About renouncing your drunken ways—'"

"The scurvy rat!" Toby snarls and charges out from behind the hedge, Fabian clutching the tails of his jacket just in time to pull him back.

"Be patient or you'll ruin everything!"

"—'As well as the fact you waste your precious time on a foolish knight—'"

"That's me, I'm sure of it!" declares Sir Andrew.

"—'One Andrew'—"

"I knew it was me!" Sir Andrew exclaims matter-of-factly. "Many call me a fool."

Noticing the letter, Malvolio stops walking and peers at the sundial. "What do we have here?" He glances around the garden, making sure he's alone…

The three onlookers duck out of sight. "The bird is nearing the trap," Fabian whispers to the others.

"'Keep quiet," Sir Toby says, "O, let him read it out loud." He crosses his fingers.

"On my life," Malvolio remarks, picking up the letter, this is my lady's handwriting! These are her C's, her U's, and her T's. And this is how she makes her long, flowing P's."

Fabian bursts out laughing but quickly throws a hand over his mouth…

"—It is her handwriting beyond question," Malvolio decides and looks more closely at the writing on the front of the letter.

"Her C's, her U's, her T's," Sir Andrew frowns, "—why would he mention that?"

"'*To the unknown beloved,*'" Malvolio reads, "'*this letter, and my sincere affection…*'" He grins. "This is precisely how she writes." Intrigued, he breaks the red wax seal and opens the letter, pausing to inspect the seal. "The impression in the wax is the very one I have seen her use for her letters! It's without doubt from my lady—but to whom has it been sent?"

"Hook, line and sinker!" Fabian says excitedly…

Intensely curious now, Malvolio begins the letter. "'*God knows I love, but who?*'" he reads. "'*Lips, do not speak the name, for no man must know my feelings yet.*' No man must know…" He ponders the phrase a moment. "What if it should be me, Malvolio," he smiles at the thought…

"Go hang yourself, vermin!" Sir Toby spits…

"'*I may command the one adored, but silence, like the sharpest knife, with bloodless wound my heart does gore. M, O, A, does rule my life.*'"

"This is gibberish!" scoffs Fabian.

"No," Sir Toby disagrees, "it's excellent work!"

"What a dish of poison she's prepared for him then."

"And how quickly he laps it up," Sir Toby comments bitterly.

"—'*I may command the one adored.*' Why, she may 'command me'. She is my lady, which is obvious to any of normal intelligence. It's not hard to see—though the last part, what does the particular arrangement of letters mean? If only I could connect that to something with me. But wait! *M.O.A.I.*" He puzzles over the significance of the letters…

"*O, I*—try and work it out, you fool!" Toby urges. "I think he's lost the scent…"

"No, the bungling bloodhound has caught a whiff of it," Fabian reasons, "—how could he *miss* it when it has the stink of fox all over it?"

"*M*—Malvolio," he says, sounding hopeful, "—the letter that begins my name."

"Didn't I tell you?" Fabian says to Sir Toby. "The dog has a nose for false scents!"

"*M*—but then the following letter breaks the pattern *A* should come next, not *O*."

"The *O* at the end of a hangman's noose would break the pattern—"

"I would beat him till he cries 'O!'" Sir Andrew speaks up defiantly.

"—And then *I* comes next," Malvolio concentrates…

"—*Aye*, it does, and if your *I* were in the back of your head, you'd see what's coming to you, sir!"

"M.O.A.I. …This puzzle is more perplexing than appeared to me at first. But if I bend it a little, I think it would yield something in the way of my understanding, for every one of these letters is *in* my name. But let's see the rest," he says and turns back to reading. "'*If this falls into your hands, ponder this. In station I am above thee, but be not afraid of greatness. Some are born great; some achieve greatness, and some have greatness thrust upon them. Fate is offering you a helping hand, so be bold and grab it with your whole heart and soul. To prepare yourself for what you are likely to become, cast off your humble self and seize upon a new one. Be direct with a certain kinsman and surly with the servants. Speak your mind about important matters—be your own unique self, one not afraid to stand out from all the others! Let she who sighs for thee give you this advice: Remember who praised you on those yellow garters you wore over your stockings, who said she would like to see them on you always? Well, you are certain of success if you want to be. If you don't, resign yourself to always being a steward, the equal of servants—one who was afraid to take Fortune's hand in your own. Farewell. She who would become your servant...* Fortunate but Unhappy.'"

Overwhelmed, Malvolio lifts his head slowly. "What could be more clear? The message is perfectly plain. I *will* stand out from others. I will read serious writers too. I will treat Sir Toby with disdain and rid myself of acquaintance with those who are beneath me. I will be exactly the kind of man she wants, down to the smallest detail." He gazes at the letter. "I'm not deceiving myself, nor letting my imagination play tricks with me. These words lead me to but one conclusion: my lady loves me." He heaves an enraptured sigh and brightens at the thought of her. "She *did* commend me recently on my cross-gartered stockings. And in this letter she shows how much she loves me by ordering me, really, to dress in a way that pleases her. I thank my *stars* that I should be so lucky! I will be more proud and aloof, and don my cross-gartered yellow stockings for her, immediately. God and my lucky stars be praised!" he cries, his attention drawn to something else in the letter. "'*P.S. You can't help but know who I am. If you accept my love, let it show in your smile. Your smiles are so... inviting. My dearest sweetheart, could I beg you to always be smiling in my presence?*'" O how I thank heaven! How I will smile! How I will make her every wish my command!" Closing his eyes, he holds the letter up to his lips and kisses it. But he breaks off when he hears a noise elsewhere in the garden. Tucking the letter inside his jacket, he turns about and rushes back toward the house, Fabian coming from behind the hedge, bursting with laughter.

"I wouldn't have missed this for a king's ransom!"

"I could marry our little villain for such handiwork!" Sir Toby cries.

"So could I," says Sir Andrew and gazes unhappily at the grass stains on the knees of his orange velvet pants.

Taking deep breaths as he regains his composure, Fabian spots Maria speeding along the path toward them. "Here comes the little devil herself."

Sir Toby gets down on his hands and knees. "Allow me to kiss those feet," he pleads, lifting his arms and bringing them down worshipfully several times.

"Allow me too," says Sir Andrew and does the same.

"May I play you at dice for my freedom, and become your slave?"

"May I be your slave too?" Sir Andrew asks, his face unsmiling.

"You've put him under such a spell that when he wakes from it he's sure to go mad."

"No," Maria says, "tell me the truth. Did it have an effect on him?"

Sir Toby bursts out laughing. "Like brandy on a child." Fabian helps him to his feet, whistling and moving his finger in crazy circles beside his head.

Maria flashes them a knowing smile. "If you want to see what comes of it, watch when he presents himself to my lady in his outrageous attire—yellow stockings, a color she utterly detests! And all the while smiling at her, which is offensive to her present mood, being given to sorrow as she is, so it can only bring him into great disgrace." She heads off. "—If you wish to see it, follow me!"

"—To the gates of hell, you most excellent devil!" Sir Toby declares loyally, throwing an arm around young Fabian's shoulder as they leave together.

"To the gates!" a frantic Sir Andrew calls behind them, his arms batting the air above his head where several wasps, attracted to his bright orange hat, are closing in….

Holding a small drum in his lap, Feste sits cross-legged on the low stone fence at the edge of Olivia's sunlit garden, tapping in time with a tune he's humming as he idly watches the comings and goings along Merchant's Row. Nothing much captures his interest for a few minutes: two children set a wagon-wheel rolling, a dog barks while chasing at their heels, a man working on the roof of a house across the way fits wooden shingles into place and nails them down…

"—God save you, friend, and your music." Feste turns to see Viola looking at him. He takes in her blue hat and satin suit, but keeps drumming. "—Do you live by your drumming?" she asks.

"No, sir," he stops drumming, "I live by the church."

"Are you a churchman then?"

"Not at all, sir. I live by the church because I live in my house, and my house is near the church."

"So you might just as well say a king lives by a beggar if a beggar lives near him: or the church stands by your drum when your drum is near the church."

"If you say so," Feste shrugs. "That's the trouble these days," he frowns, "a simple sentence is much like a glove." He raises his hands and mimes putting one on. "Yet how quickly some will turn it inside out." He lowers his middle finger, holding it down with his thumb, and shows her the rest of his fingers…

"That they can," she says as he goes back to drumming, "or perhaps it's that those who make a practice of trifling with words know how to make them seem that way."

"What way?"

"Indecent."

"Therefore, I would wish my sister had no name."

"And why is that, sir?"

"Why, sir, her name is a word. And to trifle with the word might make her seem indecent. But then, words haven't been worth much since people started swearing by them."

"What reason do you have for saying that?"

"In truth, sir, I can't give you one without words, and words are worth so little these days that I'm reluctant to use them to explain the reason they're worthless."

"I can see you are a merry fellow and care for nothing."

"Not so, sir. I do care for something. But to be honest, sir, I don't much care for you. If that means I care for nothing, I wish you were invisible."

"Aren't you the Lady Olivia's fool?"

"No, indeed, sir. The Lady Olivia has no fool, and she won't have one until she has a husband, for fools are as like husbands as sardines are like herring—the husband's the bigger one. Indeed, I am not her fool but rather her trifler with words," he says, raising his nose and affecting a lofty tone.

"I saw you recently at Count Orsino's."

"Foolery, sir, covers much ground. Like the sun: it shines everywhere. I would be sorry to see as much foolishness in your master as I do in my mistress because of you." He looks her up and down. "Methinks I did see your wise young self at the Duke's…"

"If all you will do is pass judgment on me," Viola says indignantly, "I'll be going." But then she remembers what a gentleman is supposed to do. "—Hold on, here's something for your time." She takes a coin from her pocket and offers it to him.

"May God, in his next supply of hair, send you a beard," Feste smiles and accepts the coin.

"If you only knew how I long for one," Viola murmurs, "…though I would not have it grow on my chin. Is your lady inside?"

Feste holds up the coin. "In truth, sir, wouldn't a pair of these work better?"

"Yes, if taken together they prompted an answer."

"One can always use some company…." He holds up the coin she gave him.

"I can't disagree," she smiles and gives him a second coin. "You beg well, sir."

"It's no great matter, begging for a beggar. They say great lovers are beggars," he remarks with a sly smile that causes Viola to blush slightly. "My lady is within, sir. I will explain to her and the servants from whence you have come. Who you are and what you want are unfortunately out of my sphere—I could say 'element', but the word is too often trifled with, is it not?" A playful wink and he slips from the fence. Ever the fool, he marches stiff-legged to the beat of his drum as he makes his way toward the house.

Viola watches him go then hops the stone fence and enters the garden. "…With the cleverness he possesses this fellow is made to be a jester," she muses and begins walking, "one who notes the mood as well as the character and station of those with whom he jests, picking his targets carefully rather than striking at everything he sees—surely a skill as difficult as the wise man's, for he has to be tactful in the foolishness he pursues, though even wise men, when they fall to playing the fool, forget their common sense—"

"—God save you, young gentleman," a voice hails from behind.

Viola turns to see Sir Toby Belch, now using a cane, wending his way toward her along the garden path, the orange-clad Sir Andrew in tow. "—And you too, sir."

"*Dieu vous garde, monsieur*," Sir Andrew repeats Sir Toby's greeting, but in French.

"*Et vous aussi, votre serviteur*," Viola continues.

Not up to her fluency, Sir Andrew is immediately self-conscious and responds in English: "I hope you are, sir. As I am yours."

"Will you approach the house, sir?" Sir Toby asks, sneaking an appraising glance at the fine quality of Viola's blue satin clothes while she and Sir Andrew shake hands. "—My niece has asked for you inside, if your business be with her."

"I am bound to your niece, sir," Viola explains, but corrects herself. "I mean, she is the reason for my visit."

"Test your legs, sir," Sir Toby pokes her with his cane. "Put them in motion."

"My legs 'under stand' me better than I understand what you mean by telling me to test my legs."

"I mean go in, sir, enter."

"I would be happy to, sir, but…" she notices Maria and Olivia—in her black veil—arriving in the garden, "it seems I will not have to. Most excellent and accomplished lady," she greets Olivia with a bow, "may the heavens rain odors upon you!"

"That youth's a regular courtier," Sir Andrew remarks jealously. "'Rain odors!' Well—"

"My message is for your ears only, my lady." Viola says to Olivia who turns to Maria, Sir Toby and Sir Andrew…

"Leave me alone to hear him," she says. Departing with the others, Sir Andrew mutters that he must use that himself some time: *Rain odors upon you, rain odors…*"

"Give me your hand, sir," Olivia says when they're alone.

Viola steps forward, offering her hand, "Your must dutiful and humble servant, madam."

"What is your name?"

"Cesario is your servant's name, fair princess."

"My servant, sir? It's a sad world if flattery can pass for a compliment. You're Count Orsino's servant."

"And he is yours," Viola comes back. "Your servant's servant is your servant, madam."

"—Well," says Olivia in an offhand manner, "I don't think about him. As for his thoughts, I wish they were empty rather than filled with me."

"Madam, my purpose is to inspire thoughts of him in you—"

"Don't," Olivia stops her. "I ordered you not to speak of him." Still holding Viola's hand, she toys with it and moves a little closer. "—Though I would welcome your rapturous overtures myself," she says and moves closer still, her veil almost touching Viola's face, "I would receive them as if they were the sweetest music."

"Sweet lady—" Viola flinches and tries to pull away, but Olivia won't let her.

"—After your last visit here I was not myself. I was frantic and confused." She pauses. "I sent my servant after you with a ring. But in so doing I fear I shamed my self, my servant and you. I expect that you will judge me harshly for forcing on you—through a shameful trick—something you knew wasn't yours." She drops Viola's hand and turns away. "What must you think of me?" she wonders, shaking her head. "—It's like you've tied my dignity to the stake and set your heart's cruelest thoughts to attacking it like a vicious pack of dogs."

"But madam—" Viola protests.

"I've said enough. A mere veil, not flesh and bone, hides my heart. I know you see through to my feelings…" She hesitates. "So will you not tell me yours?"

Viola hesitates before speaking. "I pity you."

"That's a step toward love," Olivia suggests hopefully.

"No, for often we pity our enemies."

"Don't say that."

"Madam—"

"Perhaps it's time to smile again," Olivia reflects. "But how proud some can be," she says in sarcasm, "as if becoming prey, I should prefer being killed by the mighty lion than the lowly wolf."

Before Viola can respond, the church tower along Merchant's Row chimes the hour.

"The clock upbraids me for wasting time," Olivia says, her voice changing tone. She turns to face Viola. "Don't worry, sir. You're not the one for me. But when you're grown and ready for harvest, your wife will reap a fine man for herself. There is the way out," she says curtly, and points across the garden, "due west."

"Then westward ho!" Viola declares quickly, "and God's blessing and grace to your ladyship." She bows to Olivia. "Will you give me no word to take back to my lord, madam?"

"Wait," Olivia says, wringing her hands in agitation. "—Before you leave," she pleads, "tell me what you think of me."

"That you think you are something you are not."

"If I think that, I think the same of you."

"Then you think right. I am not what I seem to be."

"I wish you could be what I *want* you to be."

"Would that be better, madam, than what I am?" Viola demands. "I hope it might be, for now you have made a fool of me!" Turning, she storms off along the garden path.

Thinking fast, Olivia throws off her black veil and goes after her. "Who would imagine scorn to be so beautiful on angry and contemptuous lips—a murderer's guilt shows not itself as clear as does my love the longer I keep it hidden!" She reaches Viola and seizes her by the arms. "Cesario! By the beauty of spring, by maidenhood, by truth and honor—by everything—I love thee! And nothing, neither all your pride, nor my own powers of sense and reason, can my passion hide—"

"—I swear to you, in all innocence," Viola protests, struggling to free herself from the smitten Olivia, "I have but one heart, one soul, one truth, and no woman, now or ever, shall know it, save I alone—and so adieu, good madam. Never more shall I visit you here, and implore loving feelings for my master dear." She backs away, turns and carries on walking.

"But say you will come again," Olivia pleads, though Viola is well along the garden path by now. "For perhaps that heart which now abhors his love…will find some cause to like it…" Tears coming, she touches her hands to the corners of her eyes and wipes them away, staring sadly at her garden as though it has lost all its beauty….

At the door to Olivia's parlor, Sir Toby and the servant Fabian are wrestling with Sir Andrew—dressed in a burgundy-coloured outfit this morning—trying to persuade him not to give up the quest for Olivia's hand in marriage. They bring him over to an armchair but no sooner is he seated than he springs to his feet and bolts for the door—Fabian running up and jumping in front of him to block the way.

"I told you, *no!*" Sir Andrew says with defiance, "I'll not stay a minute longer."

Sir Toby comes over. "But why, my angry friend, tell us *why* you would be leaving."

"You should at least tell us, Sir Andrew," Fabian presses.

"Well," Sir Andrew explains to Sir Toby, "I saw your niece showing the count's servant more favor than she ever thought of showing me. I saw them together in the garden."

"But did *she* see *you?*" Sir Toby inquires with a frown.

"As plain as I see you now," Sir Andrew nods.

"Well," Fabian intercedes, "*this* is proof that she loves you."

"—By God, are you trying to make an ass of me?" Sir Andrew flares in frustration, leaping up from his chair.

"I'll prove it's true, sir," Fabian offers calmly, "and on the sworn testimony of both reason and common sense." He looks to Sir Toby.

"—And they've been the best evidence since before Noah took up sailing," Sir Toby adds importantly, throwing Fabian a questioning look behind Sir Andrew's back. Fabian holds up a finger and points to himself: *Leave it to me…*

"She showed the young man more favor in front of you," he explains, "only to make you jealous, to perk up your valor, sir, to put a fire in you and start the passions burning. You should have pressed yourself upon her right then, and with some choice banter, plucked fresh from your imagination, you would have left her speechless and smitten with you. This was what you should have done, but you've missed your chance now. You let a golden opportunity slip through your fingers and now you're left out in the cold—where you'll hang like an icicle on a Dutchman's beard unless you redeem yourself with some noteworthy act of valor, or a shrewdly crafted scheme."

"If it's going to be anything, it will have to be with valor. I'm no good at schemes," Sir Andrew confesses.

"So put your fortunes in the hands of your valor then," Sir Toby urges with an emphatic gesture of his hand. "Challenge the count's youth to a fight. Hurt him in eleven or twelve places with your sword. My niece will hear of it. And I can assure you, friend, there's nothing more attractive to a woman than a man who has a reputation for valor."

"It's the only way, Sir Andrew," Fabian says.

Sir Andrew thinks for a moment. "Will one of you take my challenge to him?"

"Yes, so go and write it up," Sir Toby tells him. "Be bold but brief.

It won't matter how witty or clever it is, just so long as it's eloquent and imaginative. You can insult him safely in writing. Call him 'boy' or 'lackey' two or three times. Fill it with lies and slander. Go! Get to work. If there's enough anger behind your words, it matters not which ones you use."

"Where will I find you?" Sir Andrew starts for the door.

"We'll come to your room when you're ready. Go!"

Sir Andrew hurries out, flustered and mumbling reminders to himself: You *boy*, you *lackey*, you *liar*..."

"He's a willing puppet in your hands, Sir Toby," Fabian chuckles.

"Willing to the tune of some three thousand ducats." Sir Toby checks the contents of a wine bottle beside the armchair but finding it empty, decides to sit down.

"We'll get a rare letter from him I don't doubt. But surely you won't deliver it for him."

"Surely I will or never trust me again. And I'll do my best to provoke the youth into replying, though it would take a team of oxen to drag them together to face each other. As for Andrew, he couldn't hurt a flea even if he wanted to."

"And the youth shows no signs of being a fighter."

Maria breezes into the room, laughing almost to the point of convulsions.

"—If you want to laugh yourselves silly, follow me! Malvolio has gone mad, for no one in his right mind would have taken so to heart the ridiculous words of the letter we dropped in his way. He's wearing yellow stockings!"

"Cross-gartered?" Sir Toby gets to his feet.

"Hideously," she nods, "like a pompous old schoolmaster. I've stalked him like a murderer to see what he would do. He's followed every suggestion I made in my letter. His face wears a permanent smile that won't be wiped off—you've never seen anything quite like it. I can hardly keep myself from throwing things at him. I know my lady will strike him, yet if she does, I wager he'll but smile the more and take it as a sign of her favor!"

"Why, let's go and see," Sir Toby breaks out laughing and the three of them head quickly for the door....

In the main part of town, not far from the harbor, Sebastian and his friend Antonio round a corner and start along the crowded street past shops, stores and stalls where business is brisk on such a beautiful day…

"—I only troubled you in the first place because you so willingly offered your help," Sebastian says. "How can I be angry that you followed me?"

"I couldn't let you go alone," Antonio says. "Plus there's our friendship—which I would do anything to preserve—and because I know how difficult and sometimes dangerous it can be for a stranger in an unknown land."

Sebastian nods to a pretty woman who gives him a coy smile as she passes.

"My good Antonio, I can offer nothing more than hearty thanks at this point. Too often good deeds are shrugged off with little or no appreciation. But if my wealth were as great as my gratitude, you would find a reward worthy of all your efforts on my behalf." He looks about the street. "So, what is there to do here? Shall we explore the town?"

"Tomorrow, sir. First we had better see about a place for you to stay."

"I'm not that tired, and it's a long time till tonight. Why don't we take in the monuments and historical sites for which the town's famous?"

But Antonio's attention is suddenly focused on a small platoon of bayonet-carrying foot soldiers approaching them on patrol. "Forgive me, sir," he tells Sebastian uneasily, "but it's unwise for me to walk these streets." He stops, takes Sebastian by the arm and turns him around so they both pretend to be looking in a shop window until the soldiers have gone by. They continue walking. "Once, in a sea fight against Orsino's ships," Antonio continues, "I did some things which made me rather notorious, so if I am spotted here, I will be arrested and thrown into jail. Or worse," he adds ominously.

"Did you kill the Duke's people?"

Antonio shakes his head. "Nothing as bad as that. Let's just say the situation became confused. Some people were hurt and some damage was done. It might have been avoided if we had repaid what we took from them, which most others did in order to buy peace of mind. I was the only one who refused, which is why, if I'm caught in this place, I stand to be punished."

"Then we shouldn't be out in the open."

"I've never been one for hiding my face," Antonio declares, and stops walking. "Here's some money." He takes a small pouch from one of his pockets and forces it on Sebastian. "The Elephant Inn on the south side of town is the best place to stay. I'll go on ahead while you spend some time getting to know the town. We'll meet later at the Inn."

"Why would I need money?" Sebastian holds up the pouch.

Antonio looks to the window of the tailor's shop in front of which they've come to stand. "It won't get you anything luxurious, but at least you'll look like the gentleman you really are."

"We'll meet in an hour then."

"At The Elephant."

They shake hands and Antonio moves off down the street, Sebastian comparing the tattered state of the clothes he's wearing, with the stylish and colorful shirts, jackets and pants on display in the window, a blue satin outfit catching his eye in particular. A bell on the door tinkling as he opens up, he smiles and goes inside....

Without her veil now, Olivia paces nervously near the standing sundial in her garden where Malvolio found Maria's letter. "I've sent for him," she murmurs to herself, "...but supposing he agrees to come, how shall I entertain him? Young affections are more often bought with *things* than they are with pleas and protestations—but I'm talking too loudly," she says uneasily, and glances at Maria. "—Where's Malvolio?"

Maria looks up from smelling some flowers. "Oh he's coming,

madam, but he's acting most strangely. Indeed, it's safe to say, he's not himself."

Olivia frowns. "Why, what's wrong?"

Maria shrugs and shakes her head.

"Has he taken to raving about something or other?" Olivia presses.

"No, madam. He does nothing but smile. I think it would be best that you have someone with you if he approaches. To all appearances, the man has lost his mind."

"Go call him here," Olivia says and turns away. Maria bows and quickly departs.

Olivia touches a hand to the pointer on the face of the sundial, lost in thought. "I am perhaps as mad as he," she reflects, "if being wracked between joy and despair is what makes for madness—how are you Malvolio?"

A blissful smile on his face, her steward is advancing along the path in his usual black clothes, but black ribbons are now wrapped in crisscross patterns over the bright yellow stockings he is wearing, pulled up over his knees. He sports a matching yellow handkerchief in the pocket of his jacket as well.

"Sweet lady," he says with a smitten sigh, "you were asking for me?" He winks and widens his smile.

"Why are you smiling? I sent for you on a serious matter."

"Serious, my lady?" He shakes his head. "I don't mind being serious, although this cross-gartering does restrict the blood supply, but what of it, if it please a certain person's eye? That is enough for me. Didn't someone once say: Please one, and you please all?"

"What?" Olivia frowns. "What's the matter with you?"

"What could be the matter, my lady, when there's yellow on my legs?" He gazes at the sundial beside her. "The order was received and the commands have been carried out. I think we understand each other, do we not?"

"Shouldn't you be in bed, Malvolio?"

"In bed?" he asks, taken aback. He starts blowing kisses. "'Yes, my sweet,' as the poet wrote, 'and I'll wait upon thee there…'"

"God love you! Why are you smiling so, and kissing your hand like that?"

"—What is wrong, Malvolio?" asks Maria, who has been looking on.

"You expect an answer to that? Does a nightingale answer a crow? Puh!" he sneers at her.

"Why are you behaving like such a fool in front of my mistress?"

"*Be not afraid of greatness,*" he quotes from the letter. "That puts it nicely."

"Puts *what* so nicely?"

"*Some are born great—*" He takes a step toward Olivia.

"For the love of God—"

"*Some achieve greatness—*" He comes closer still.

"What are you *doing?*" She glares in disbelief.

"*And some have greatness thrust upon them.*" He reaches out and takes her hand between his own as if to kiss it.

"—Heaven *help* you!" Olivia cries and pulls away from him.

"*Remember who praised your yellow stockings—*" He plucks the yellow handkerchief from his pocket and waves it in the air.

"—Yellow stockings?"

"*And wished to see you always cross-gartered—*" He stalks forward.

"—Wished to *see* you?" She retreats.

"*You are certain of success if you want to be—*" He continues stalking her.

"—*I* am certain of success?" she backs toward Maria.

"*If not, stay a steward forever—*" he declares and rushes forward to embrace her.

"—This is perfect madness!" She ducks quickly behind Maria, who crosses her arms and keeps the smiling Malvolio at bay. A servant appears behind him on the path and, with an amused glance at the bright yellow stockings and black garters, presents himself to Olivia.

"Madam, Count Orsino's young gentleman has returned. It was with some difficulty I persuaded him to, but he awaits your ladyship's pleasure."

"I'll come to him," Olivia says, relieved to be going. "Good Maria, see that this fellow is cared for." She starts along the path. "Where is Sir Toby?"

"I couldn't say, madam."

"He and some of my servants can take special care of him. On my fortune, I don't want to see him get hurt…"

"No, madam," says Maria, suppressing a smile as she hastens away, turning for a last look at Malvolio who is twirling on his toes in the rapture of true love.

"O, you do understand me after all," he rejoices. "No less a man than Sir Toby to care for me, exactly the words of her letter. She sends him on purpose, so that I may act rudely to him. That is what she encouraged me to in the letter. 'Cast off your modest ways,' she said. 'Be obstinate with a certain kinsman, and surly with the servants. Speak out on important topics. Be yourself!' And after that, described precisely how it should be done: a serious face," he puts one on, "a dignified walk," he postures and takes a few steps, "—talking slowly, wearing clothes suitable to some important gentleman, and so on," he waves the yellow handkerchief gaily. "I've caught her!" he beams in jubilation. "Although it's heaven's doing," he concedes, putting on a solemn face, "and heaven make me thankful. For to say, as she did just now, 'Let this *fellow* be cared for.' 'Fellow'! Not 'Malvolio.' Not 'steward.' But 'fellow'! Why, everything fits, so that no shadow of a doubt, no shadow of a shadow, no obstacle, impediment or threatening circumstance—what more can be said? Nothing can come between me, and the fulfillment of my hopes. …Well, heaven, not I, has done this, and heaven is to be thanked." A prayerful smile on his face, he bows his head…

"Where is he, in the name of all that's holy?" Sir Toby booms on his way into the garden with Maria and Fabian. "Even if all the devils in hell have possessed him—or Satan himself has taken over his soul, I want to speak with him!"

"Over there," Maria points left at a fork in the path and steers them toward the sundial.

Fabian scoots ahead on the path and soon spots Malvolio. "Here he is, over here…" He slows his pace and approaches cautiously. "How are you feeling, sir?"

"How are you, man?" Sir Toby asks, frowning as though gravely concerned.

Malvolio halfway turns his head. "Go away," he sneers. "I have no business with you. Let me enjoy my privacy. Go away!"

"How deep the devil has gone inside him!" exclaims Maria. "—Sir Toby, my lady begs you to see that he's cared for."

"Ah ha!" Malvolio interjects, grinning. "Does she indeed…"

"I most certainly will," Sir Toby solemnly assures her, "I most certainly will. *Shh!*" he puts a finger to his lips, "we must be gentle with him. Leave him to me." He steps up to Malvolio. "How is it with you, sir? Bollocks, man, renounce the devil if you know what's good for you. Remember," he shifts his eyes and look around. "—He's the enemy of us all!"

Malvolio gapes in disbelief. "Do you know what you're saying?"

"Look!" Maria points out. "He takes offence when you speak ill of the devil! Pray God he's not been bewitched!"

"Send for the exorcist," Fabian suggests, a worried look on his face.

"First thing tomorrow, it will be done" Maria nods and then clutches the sleeve of Sir Toby's jacket. "My lady would not lose him for more than I can say."

"What's that, madam?" Malvolio pricks up his ears.

"O Lord!" Maria wails suddenly, and bursts into tears.

"Hush, madam," Sir Toby puts a comforting arm around her shoulder. "This is *not* the way. Can't you see you're upsetting him? Let me deal with him…" He gestures for Malvolio to let him have the yellow handkerchief to give to Maria, but he holds it close and shakes his head in refusal.

"—Gentleness is the only way," Fabian advises. "The devil is rough and won't be treated roughly." He reaches out his hand to pat Malvolio on the head. "Gently, very gent—"

"—Sir!" Malvolio objects and bats away his arm, unaware that Sir Toby has come up behind and taken him firmly in hand.

"—Now, now, come along," Sir Toby says gently and leads Malvolio off. "—It's beneath the dignity of a man in your position to play games like this, sir…"

"Have him say his prayers," pleads Maria.

"My prayers!" Malvolio sneers disdainfully—but sees his chance and wriggles out from under the arm Sir Toby has around his shoulders.

"No!" Maria cries after him, "I fear he's too far gone for prayer!"

"Go hang yourselves, you idle and shallow things!" Malvolio shouts back at them as he flees toward the house. "—You shall hear more of this! *I promise you!*"

"Can it be?" Sir Toby says and dissolves in a fit of laughter.

"—No one would believe this unless they saw it with their own eyes!" Fabian hoots, doubled-over with laugher.

"—He's completely fallen for it," says Sir Toby, his laughter easing off.

"But you should keep after him in case it comes to light that he's been tricked," suggests Maria.

"We could drive him out of his mind, if we had a mind to," Fabian jokes.

"The house would be quieter without him," Maria says.

Sir Toby gathers them around. "Here's what should be done, then. With his hands tied behind him, we place him in a dark room. My niece is well on her way to believing he's mad. Thus we can keep him penned up—for our amusement as well as his punishment—until we've had enough, or we start to feel sorry for him, at which point we'll own up to the scheme," he winks at Maria, "and crown this dear woman queen of the madhouse!—But who do we have here?"

Sir Andrew Aguecheek, in an emerald-green velvet outfit, hat and shoes, is striding toward them along the garden path.

"More madness for a May morning…" Fabian quips.

"Here's the challenge," Sir Andrew grins, and holds up a sheet of paper. "Read it. I guarantee there's pith and vinegar in it!"

"You don't thay," Fabian quips. Maria rolls her eyes.

"Yes, there truly is. Just read it!"

"Let me see," Sir Toby says and takes it from him. "'Youth, whoever you may be,'" he reads, "'you are a vile and contemptible fellow.'"

"It's bold, I'll say that," Fabian nods.

"'Be not amazed,'" Sir Toby continues, "'nor marvel not in your mind as to why I would call you that, for I will show no reason for it.'"

"A good point," Fabian comments, "to avoid charges of slander."

Pleased with himself, Sir Andrew smiles.

"'You come to see the Lady Olivia, and right in front of me she treats you with affection. But you lie through your teeth, sir, and that is not the reason I am challenging you.'"

"Very brief, and sens—" Fabian corrects himself, "—less."

"'I will waylay you as you go home, and if by chance you kill me—'"

"Good," says Fabian.

" '—You would kill me like a rogue and a villain.'"

"You're still on the safe side of the law, good," Fabian says.

"'Farewell, and God have mercy on one of our souls! He may have mercy on mine, but my hope for survival is better, so protect your self! Your friend, if you treat him so, and your sworn enemy. Sir Andrew Aguecheek.'" Sir Toby looks over the letter. "If this doesn't move him, then nothing will. I'll give it to him."

"Well, your opportunity may come sooner than you think," Maria says, "for he's conversing with my lady as we speak—by now on the verge of leaving." She gives him an encouraging look, then turns to head into the house.

"Go, Sir Andrew, and keep an eye out for him at the corner of the garden," Sir Toby advises. "As soon as you see him, draw your sword, and as you draw, swear and denounce him. For it often happens that an angry oath, spoken with bravado, attests to a man's valor more than the actual performance of some act. —Off you go!"

"Leave the swearing to me!" Sir Andrew declares with a defiant look on his face, pushing the hair out of his eyes with one hand and planting the other on the handle of his sword as he charges off through the garden.

Sir Toby lets out a sigh. "There is no way I can deliver the letter," he confides to Fabian, "since the youth's behavior shows him to be a person of quality and breeding. His employment as messenger between Orsino and my niece confirms it. This letter," he holds it up, "being the work of none but an idiotic mind, will leave the youth in stitches of laughter rather than running for his life, for it's clearly written by a blockhead. I'll deliver the challenge by word of mouth instead, giving Aguecheek such a fearsome reputation for fighting the young gentleman—being inexperienced in these matters and more apt to be overwhelmed—will be shocked by the details of his temper, rage and fury. They'll both be so frightened when they meet, one will kill the other with just a look—"

Noticing something, Fabian pulls Sir Toby aside and points across the garden to the front door of the house where Olivia is bidding Viola goodbye. "—There he is with your niece. Let's wait till he leaves and then go after him."

"Meanwhile I'll come up with a decent challenge," Sir Toby declares and goes off into the garden, leaving Fabian to keep his eyes on Olivia and Viola by the front door...

"—I have said so much to a heart of stone," Olivia confesses. "And I've carelessly risked my honor by doing so. There is something in me that hates what I've done, but the urge is so stubborn and powerful within me that I'm helpless to control it."

"My master's grief beats this way in his heart, as passion does in yours," Viola responds.

"—Here..." Olivia removes a silver locket and chain from around her neck. "Wear this for me. It has my picture in it." Viola shakes her head *No* and steps back. "Don't refuse it. It has no tongue to upset you. And I beg you to come again tomorrow." She glances at the locket in her hand then meets Viola's eyes. "What could you ask of me that I would not give if I could do so honorably?"

"Only this: your true love for my master."

"How can I honorably give him that which I have given to you?"

"I forgive you every word you've said to me."

Nothing to be done, Olivia gives an appreciative nod. "Well, come again tomorrow," she says. " Farewell. A devil that looked like you could carry me off to hell," she smiles self-consciously and goes inside.

Viola turns and is making for the street when she notices Sir Toby gesturing urgently at her from the garden.

"Gentleman, God save you!" he calls, waving her over.

"And you, sir," she replies, approaching the gate. He holds it open and then follows her into the garden where, a worried look on his face, he pulls her quickly aside.

"Whatever skill you have as a swordsman, be prepared to use it," he warns, speaking fast and glancing warily around the garden as he talks. "I don't know what you've done to upset him, but your adversary—

filled with hatred and out for blood—awaits you at the other end of the garden. Draw your sword and stand ready, for your assailant is skillful, blood-thirsty and deadly."

"I'm sure you must be mistaken, sir," Viola protests. "No man has any argument with me. I have no recollection of having quarreled with anyone."

"I think otherwise, sir. Therefore, if you value your life, you'd best prepare to defend yourself, for your opponent has all that youth, strength, skill and anger can give him."

"My opponent? What opponent?"

"He is a knight, sir, although of the ceremonial order rather than the battlefield, but still he's a devilish strong fighter. He's killed three men, and he is at the moment so enraged that nothing will satisfy him except a fatal wound that leads to your death. "'To have or have not', is his motto: *kill or be killed.*"

Frightened, Viola turns back toward the gate. "—I will return to the house and ask the lady for some protection. I am no fighter. I have heard of men picking quarrels with others in order to test their valor, no doubt this is a man of that type."

"—No, sir, his anger stems from something you've done to him," Sir Toby explains. "You'd best go deal with him now, before his anger explodes and he comes looking for you. Besides, you can't go back to the house without getting past me, which would be almost as bad as facing him," and with his bulky body he blocks the way. "Get going, or draw your sword and fight me. For duel you must—or never call yourself a man again."

"This is as improper as it is strange," she responds, letting his last remark pass. "I beg you for a favor—could you ask the knight how I have offended him?"

"I could," Sir Toby nods.

"It can only be something that happened by accident, nothing I would have done on purpose," she offers in dismay.

"Master Fabian!" Sir Toby calls, and Fabian emerges from his hiding place in the shrubs close by. "Stay with this gentleman until I get back." He bids Viola farewell then with a determined look on his face hastens off toward the other end of the garden.

"—Please, sir," Viola appeals to Fabian, "do you know what's going on?"

Fabian shrugs. "I know the knight is so angry with you he wants a duel to the death. But more than that I couldn't say."

"What kind of man is he?" she asks uneasily.

"To judge by his appearance," Fabian says matter-of-factly, "there are no outward indications of what you would face in testing his valor. However, he's rumored to be the most daring, violent and deadly opponent you'll find anywhere in Illyria." He notices Viola's mounting terror. "If you wished to come and meet him, I could endeavor to make peace with him on your behalf." He puts out his arm, showing her the way.

"I would be most grateful for that, sir," she says, and they begin walking. "I am a person who would much rather deal with a reverend priest than a titled knight—and I don't care who knows that about me," Viola explains, hurrying to keep up with the speedy Fabian...

Sir Toby leads Sir Andrew Aguecheek to an open area near the low stone fence that runs beside the street, the tall knight's eyes growing wider as he listens to Sir Toby elaborating on the danger he's in. "The word I would use to describe him is *livid*, sir. I've never seen such a temper in all my life. I myself had a run-in with him, swords out and all, and before I could raise my blade he had his point against my throat with such accuracy, I couldn't swallow until he took the blade away. And my return thrust he batted away like it was nothing. —They say he has been a fencer for the shah of Persia."

"That does it!" Sir Andrew bursts, "I'll not fight with him."

"But sir, it's too late to try and appease him now. Fabian can scarcely hold him back."

"That does it! If I knew he was so fierce, and such a daring fighter, I would have let myself be damned before I'd have challenged him as I have done." He clutches the lapels of Sir Toby's jacket. "—If he'd let the matter go I would gladly give him my best horse, gray Capulet."

Sir Toby makes a face and deliberates with himself. "I suppose I could make an offer." Sir Andrew offers a pleading glance. "Very well," Sir Toby gives way. "Stand here and act as though you won't be toyed with. I hope we can bring this to an end without loss of life. Indeed," he chuckles to himself as he marches off, "I'll ride that gray horse as well as I ride you..." But the next moment he stops walking: Fabian and Viola are approaching up ahead. Seeing Sir Toby they halt, Fabian instructing Viola to wait where she is while he goes over to meet with Sir Toby.

"He's promised me his best horse for settling this quarrel," Sir Toby whispers gleefully when he and Fabian put their heads together. "—I've persuaded him the youth's a blood-thirsty devil."

"—The gentleman's just as frightened of him," Fabian chuckles. "He's white as a ghost and shaking like he's just seen one."

Sir Toby concludes the tête-à-tête with a solemn nod for appearances' sake then carries on down the path toward Viola. "There's no other choice, sir," he tells her. "He still has to fight with you over the matter of his honor, however he's considered the issue he has with you, and he wonders if an all-out duel is what's required to give him satisfaction. Therefore, draw your sword, so he can save face, but he promises he won't hurt you." He helps Viola take out her sword and hold it up, which she does using two hands.

"Pray God defend me!" she tells herself as Sir Toby walks back to consult with Sir Andrew. "—It wouldn't take much for me to confess I am not a man."

"Give way if you see him getting too angry," says Fabian who comes up beside Viola and shows her how to hold the sword...

Sir Toby charges up to Sir Andrew near the low stone fence where he's been frantically pacing. "There's no other way, sir. The gentleman insists on one bout with you for honor's sake. By the code of dueling, he has no choice. But he's promised me, as a gentleman and a soldier, that he won't hurt you. Come on, go to it." He takes Sir Andrew by the arm and leads him forward.

"Pray God he keeps his promise!" says Sir Andrew, and reluctantly draws his sword.

Fabian advancing on the garden path with Viola, she readies her sword. "I assure you, sir, it's against my will to be doing this," she tells him.

"Put up your swords!" a voice suddenly shouts from the street: Sebastian's friend Antonio jumps over the stone fence and confronts Sir

Andrew. "If this young gentleman has offended you, I will answer for it. If you have offended him, I will challenge you on his behalf." He reaches for Viola's sword then waves it so skillfully in the air that Sir Andrew's jaw drops in frightened astonishment.

"Who are you, sir?" Sir Toby demands and moves in front of Sir Andrew.

"One, sir, who for love of this young man will dare do even more than he has bragged to you he will."

"Well, if you're so eager to meet your maker, I'm for you!" Sir Toby declares as he pulls out and brandishes his sword, but Fabian, having noticed something in the street, tries to get him to put it down.

"Here come the officers, Sir Toby!"

At the head of a platoon of soldiers, the first officer takes out his sword and gives the order for his men to do the same then waves his second officer to follow him into the garden.

"Don't move," Sir Toby points his finger at Antonio and goes to confront the officers as they come over the fence...

Still facing each other on the path, Viola pleads with Sir Andrew. "Please, sir, put your sword away if you would."

"Indeed I will, sir," Andrew replies looking relieved, and does so. "And about the matter of my horse, I'll be as good as my word."

"'The matter of the horse'?" Viola asks with a puzzled frown.

Sir Andrew nods, a sorry look on his face. "He's a smooth ride that horse, and easy to manage besides..."

"—This is the man," the first officer says and pushes past Sir Toby. "Do your duty" Sword out, his second officer seizes Antonio by the arm.

"—I arrest you in the name of Count Orsino."

"You've mistaken me for someone else," Antonio calmly tells the officer.

"No, sir," the first officer shoots back, "I'd know you anywhere, even without your captain's hat. Take him away," he snaps at the second officer. "He knows I know him well."

Antonio makes no comment but turns to Viola. "This comes from seeking you." The officer pulls him to go but he resists. "There's no way round it," he says to Viola, "I'll take what's coming to me. —But what will you do, since I have to ask for my purse back? The thought of being unable to help you saddens me more than the thought of what will happen to me." Viola gapes at him, bewildered. "—Why do you look at me that way? It's not the worst that could befall me."

"Come, sir,," the officer barks beside him.

Still refusing to go, Antonio reaches out to Viola. "I must beg you for some of my money back—"

"What money?" she asks. "In return for the generous kindness you've shown me? I don't see that as called for. However, considering your present trouble, I will lend you something. I don't have much, but I could share it with you." She takes out her pouch, shakes the contents into the palm of her hand and takes three of her six gold coins. "Here's half of all I have in the world."

"How can you deny me like this?" Antonio demands, glaring in disbelief. "—Have you forgotten all I've done for you? The help I've given—the kindnesses I've shown you?"

"I know of none, sir," Viola replies innocently. "Nor do I recognize anything about you. I hate ingratitude as much as the next man—more than lies and deceit, or any other vice of human nature, but—"

"Think again! " Antonio pleads.

"Come, sir," the officer snarls and forces him to start walking.

"—Let me speak," he protests and stands his ground, his eyes on Viola. "This youth I rescued when he was half-drowned. Cared for and tended to him night and day until his injuries were healed, and in so doing came to revere the courage he showed in the face of tragedy—a more devoted friend I couldn't have been."

"What's that to us?" scoffs the first officer. "We're wasting time. Let's go!"

"O how faithless you have proven yourself, Sebastian!" Antonio cries as he's helped over the fence and led away. "—What empty lies are behind that virtuous image you present to the world!" he shouts, struggling with the soldiers who are now surrounding him in the street. "—How beauteous evil can appear when the devil is at work within—"

"This is madness—away with him!" the first officer shouts, and the soldiers move out in two columns, a disheartened Antonio turning his head as he trudges between them.

"Sebastian!" he calls back over his shoulder, "Sebastian!"

Stepping up to the stone fence, Viola watches him go. "His words from such great passion fly, that he believes them true," she murmurs, "and so would I. O that they might prove true," she pleads, "that I, dear brother, am mistaken for you!"

Behind her, Sir Toby takes Fabian and Sir Andrew aside. "—A word or two, gentlemen…"

"He called me Sebastian," Viola muses to herself, "—who is alive still, when I see myself in the mirror. His features very like my own, his clothes of this same color, fashion and style as I wear. —I've left off being myself and now am he. …If only it were true—that there is kindness in storms after all, and bounteous love in the wildness of the sea."

She hops nimbly over the stone fence and ventures into the street while the three men are still talking, Sir Toby the first to notice she's gone.

"A damned dishonorable and contemptible boy!" he curses, "running off like this! A coward through and through—deserting his friend in his hour of need. Is he not Fabian?"

"No question," Fabian pipes up at a nudge from Sir Toby. "He's a devout coward, sir," he affirms for Sir Andrew, "as wholly a coward as I've ever seen. Why you might even call him—" Sir Toby draws a finger across his throat—*Enough!*

"—By God," Sir Andrew declares hotly, "I'll go and thrash him for it, *that's* what I'll do!"

"Do it, sir," Toby urges. "Thrash him soundly.? But not with your sword."

"If I don't—" Sir Andrew charges forward and, in a flurry of limbs, takes the fence in a single bound, the rest of his words lost as he lopes down the street after Viola.

"Come, sir," Fabian sighs, "we'd best go and see what happens."

"I'll wager it won't be much," Sir Toby groans, clambering over the fence. "Not much at all…" Fabian joins him, and they start off along Merchant's Row….

Fresh from the tailor shop in his stylish new clothes and hat, Sebastian emerges from The Elephant Inn and casts his eyes around the busy street as though looking for someone. He decides on a direction and moves off along the road beside the harbor, searching the faces of passersby as he goes, peering into the windows of stores and shops in case Antonio is there.

Stopping at the corner where the harbor street intersects with Merchant's Row, he waits with the other pedestrians while several open carriages go past, the noise of clopping horses and clattering wheels filling the street for a moment before an attractive young woman standing next to Sebastian catches his eye with a flirting smile that shows she's very taken with him in his handsome blue outfit, a sword and dagger with matching silver handles at his waist.

He returns her smile but with little interest then discreetly turns his eyes away, peering across the road until, having nowhere else to look without meeting her eyes again, he glances down at the street—a white handkerchief floating to the ground a moment later so it lands at his feet.

He looks up and the young woman widens her smile. With the people around them about to start moving again, Sebastian crouches down quickly and retrieves the handkerchief, unaware that as he's doing so, the platoon escorting Antonio is marching by, the second officer marking time for his soldiers: *Hup, hup, hup-hup-hup…*

Standing up, Sebastian returns the handkerchief. The young woman meets his glance with a look that says she would like to linger for a conversation…but an older woman beside her—her mother by the looks of it—takes her arm and starts them across the street, Sebastian staying where he is until they are well down the next block and the young woman has stopped looking back at him.

Suddenly a hand reaches up from behind and grabs him by his ponytail. Sebastian turns and shoots a look at old Feste who holds up the money-purse he's just picked from his pocket.

Sebastian grabs for his money but Feste keeps it out of reach and, thinking it's Cesario he's dealing with, takes him by the arm and is heading him up Merchant's Row when Sebastian lunges for his money-purse, but he's not fast enough: Feste keeps it out of reach and continues walking. "—Are you telling me I *wasn't* sent to find you and bring you home?"

"You're looking for trouble where there isn't any, sir," Sebastian warns. "Give me the purse then leave me alone." Feste stops walking, pulls out the lining of his pants' pockets and holds up his hands to show that he no longer has the purse. He whistles and points for Sebastian to check his jacket pocket: he does, and pulls out the money-purse.

Sebastian glares coldly then starts back toward Harbor Street, Feste running up in front of him, turning with a deft pirouette and walking backwards while he talks.

"—You put on a good act, sir, I'll give you that." He studies Sebastian's face. "No, I don't know you then. *Nor* was I sent by my lady to ask you to return and speak with her, *nor* is your name Cesario, nor is *this*," he points, "the nose on my face. Nothing that is so, is so, is that it?"

"Vent your foolishness somewhere else," Sebastian sneers and pushes past him. "—You don't know me."

"'*Vent*' my foolishness?" Feste laughs and turns away, as if talking to someone behind him. "He's heard his betters use the word and now has a chance to employ it—though it takes a deal more than fancy words to fool a fool like me…" He stops walking, levels his eyes and plants a hand on Sebastian's chest. "—Look, sir, enough of this game. Just tell me what it is I shall 'vent' to my lady. Shall I 'vent' that you will come or not?"

"Enough is right!" cries Sebastian. But each time he tries to get past

Feste, the old fool blocks his way. "All right!" Sebastian finally gives up. "Here's something for you." He takes several coins from the money-purse and tosses them at Feste who catches them with no trouble. "Now make yourself scarce or you'll get worse payment than that."

"My word," Feste remarks, glancing at the gold in his hand, "you're most generous this time."

"'This time'?" Sebastian looks puzzled.

"Now I see how a wise man builds his reputation," Feste quips, "by giving fools money, and plenty of it!" But he frowns uneasily as he's pocketing his take and directs Sebastian's eyes to Merchant's Row where a belligerent-looking Andrew Aguecheek is coming up fast, Fabian and Sir Toby not far behind.

"Ah ha, sir!" Sir Andrew calls when he spots Sebastian. "—We meet again!" He charges forward and removes his green leather gloves. "Here's something for you!" he declares brashly, and slaps Sebastian across the face with his gloves.

Sebastian reacts instantly, drawing his dagger and holding it by the blade. "—And here's something for you!" He raps Aguecheek on the side of the head with the polished silver handle then strikes again to the other side of the head. "—And this!" He pokes it in Andrew's stomach. "—And this!" When Aguecheek looks down, flustered by the attack, Sebastian brings the handle up and is about to hit him under the chin when Sir Toby steps in and seizes him by the wrist.

"—Enough, sir! Put your weapon away or I'll do it for you."

"Have all you people gone mad?" demands Sebastian, wrestling with Sir Toby over the dagger.

"I'd better inform my lady, and quickly too," Fabian decides. "—I wouldn't give a fortune to be in your shoes, Sir Toby!" he calls and goes running up Merchant's Row as the grappling continues.

"Stop it, sir, if you know what's good for you," Sir Toby grunts.

"I have it!" Sir Andrew pipes up, "I'll get him some other way. I'll have him charged with assault—there must be laws in Illyria," he looks to Sir Toby, "and though I struck first, I used no weapon, just as you told me."

"—Let me go!" Sebastian shouts, but Sir Toby has him in a headlock.

"—I told you, sir, I will not let you go until you throw the dagger down. You drew first blood as they say—come now!"

"I'll be free of you!" says Sebastian and drops the dagger as ordered, Sir Toby loosening his grip in order to kick it out of harm's way—but Sebastian breaks free and draws his sword. "What do you say now, sir?" An accomplished swordsman, he flicks the weapon a few times in Sir Toby's face then finishes with a move that places the sharp tip against the older man's big barrel chest. "—Only a madman would dare draw his sword now," he says threateningly.

"Then call me mad," Sir Toby declares, "but I think I'll see what that bold blood in you is made of." He pulls out his sword and they go to it, Sebastian the better fighter but Sir Toby giving as good as he gets so the clash of metal rises in the street and a crowd begins to form, Sir Andrew silently cheering on his friend, though in his excitement he brings his gloves down one too many times on the head of the man in front of him—a short fellow—who glares, offended, and grabs the gloves away from a scared-looking Aguecheek at the same time as the crowd turns to watch a carriage hurtling down Merchant's Row toward them.

"—No, Sir Toby!" Olivia shouts, on her feet in the back of the carriage. And when her driver brings it to a stop a moment later she climbs quickly down and storms into the crowd, people making way for her as she passes. "In the name of decency, I order you to put your weapon down!" she rails at her uncle.

With Sebastian lowering his sword, Sir Toby does the same, throwing his niece a perturbed look.

"Madam—" he begins to say, but she cuts him off, her body shaking she is so upset.

"You boorish and unruly man!" she lambastes him. "Is there no stopping this gross, outlandish behavior? You're not fit to live among civilized people! Get out of my sight! Go!"

Beaten but unbowed, Sir Toby throws Sebastian a sullen sneer then turns and goes, Aguecheek following meekly behind him, the crowd dispersing quietly, disappointed that the fight is over.

Olivia waits till she and Sebastian are alone. "—If I could entreat your forgiveness for my uncle's sorry behavior," she offers in apology,

"…have you hold your anger in abeyance and come along with me so I can redeem myself in some way," she gives him a hopeful smile, "perhaps regale you with stories of my uncle's antics more unbelievable than what you witnessed here—through which you might even come to see the lighter side of this lady," she says good-naturedly. "You *must* come to my house," she insists warmly and looks with affection into his eyes, more enthralled with him than ever.

Bewildered, Sebastian begs a moment for himself and starts looking for his hat. "Things grow stranger by the minute," he says under his breath. "What shall I tell her?" He spots his hat and walks over to pick it up. "—Either I've gone completely mad or this is some incredible dream I am having." He puts on his hat and watches as Olivia waves for her driver to bring the carriage over: dressed beautifully and without her veil, she is a radiant and stunning woman. Sebastian, gazing at her, is spellbound. "May imagination prove I'm not mistaken," he decides, "—if this is a dream, never let me waken…"

"Now, sir," she resumes the conversation, "do you propose to join me?"

"Madam, I do," he replies.

"…And soon I hope to say so too," she murmurs, a touch of coyness in the happy smile on her face as he offers his hand and helps her into the carriage, which the driver turns in the direction of Merchant's Row, Olivia and Sebastian close together in the seat, their eyes only for each other.…

Their faces glowing in light from the candles they're holding, Feste and Maria are careful on the dark stairs leading down to Olivia's cellar, Maria quick to hand over the bundle of clothes she has with her once they reach the bottom.

"Put on this robe and beard to make him believe you're Father Topas, the righteous parson," she whispers. "I'll go fetch Sir Toby." Feste sets his candle down and accepts the clothes. The robe is fine, but the long gray beard? He shoots her a look. "It's the best I could do," she says, and with a shrug turns to go back upstairs…

Feste sighs and shakes his head. "Well, why not. I wouldn't be the first person that ever hid behind robes and a beard." He slips the vestment over his head, realizing that with the cowl bunching up under his chin he's put it on back-to-front. Turning it around, he moves closer to the candle and considers his disguise. "If I were taller I'd doubtless make a righteous parson, if thinner a great scholar." He chuckles at himself and peers into the darkness. "—Though, come to think of it, I'd just as soon have them say I was a decent man or a pleasant companion, as I would that I was a righteous parson or a great scholar—" He holds the beard up in the candlelight and winces squeamishly: gray and full as well as being long, it looks as if it's only recently been clipped from a man's chin. He finally brings himself to try it on, noticing as he does so that candles have appeared at the top of the stairs: Maria and Sir Toby. "Descend fellow conspirators," he intones as he makes minor adjustments to his beard by the light of the candle…

Sir Toby huffs and puffs as he arrives at the bottom of the stairs and takes in Feste's disguise, to which he gives an approving nod. All ready, Marie signals the two men to begin.

"—Welcome and God bless you, Father Topas," Sir Toby says in a solemn voice.

"*Bonos dies*," Feste responds somberly, in botched Latin, though his lofty tone is that of the devoutly religious man. "…For as the old hermit of Prague, who never used pen and ink in his life, remarked to a niece of King Gorbuduc's out of the blue one day, 'That that is, is.'" He speaks the words as though they are the most profound in all philosophy. "So I, being *Father Topas*," he emphasizes the name, "am *Father Topas*. For what is '*that*' but '*that*'? And what is '*is*' but '*is*'?" He strokes his beard sagely and looks to the others to see if they're as pleased with his performance as he is.

Maria rolling her eyes, Sir Toby frowns and waves impatiently for him to get moving. "—Go to him, Father Topas…"

Winking, Feste pulls the cowl over his head, takes up his candle and, holding it out in front of him, advances slowly through the darkness: wooden barrels, casks and trunks, rusted anchors, chains and coils of rope briefly visible in the candlelight as he passes on his way to the padlocked door of another room which has a small, grille-covered opening in it at eye level. Feste lifts his candle up and peers through the bars of the grille. "Hark, I say…" He listens for a moment, someone stirring inside the room. "—Peace to you in your prison," he calls.

Enjoying himself, Sir Toby turns to Maria. "—The rascal does a good job, does he not?" She shrugs and sits down on the stairs; he takes a flask from the pocket of his jacket and drinks.

"—Who is there?" Malvolio cries inside the room, his face faintly illuminated by the flickering candle as he presses it to the grille..

"It is I, Father Topas," Feste declares solemnly, "—come to visit Malvolio the lunatic."

"Father Topas!" Malvolio rejoices at the sound of the name. "Good Father Topas, you must go to my lady for me—"

"—Out, you diabolical fiend!" Feste erupts suddenly. "How you torment this man—he can talk of nothing besides women!"

"Nicely done, Topas," Sir Toby chuckles and has another drink.

"—O Father Topas," protests Malvolio, "no man has ever been so mistreated as I. Good Father Topas, please don't think me mad. They have confined me here in hideous darkness—"

"Darkness? Fire and brimstone, you shameless—" he can't think of anything, "—*shameless* man! Did you call this house 'dark'?"

"As hell, Father Topas."

"Why, its broad bay windows are translucent as walls of stone," he objects, "and the upper levels facing south-north-south, are as bright as blackest ebony. Yet you complain there's no light?"

"I complain that I am cooped up here when I am not mad, Father Topas. This house is dark I tell you."

"Madman, you are mistaken. Father Topas knows it is not darkness by which you are confounded, but *ignorance*," he emphasizes, "as the Egyptians were till they thought of the pyramids."

"I tell you this house is as dark as ignorance," Malvolio insists, "—darker than the ignorance of hell itself. And I tell you, no man was ever so abused as I—I am no more a madman than you are." A moot point with Feste, he makes a face and chortles. "—Put me to the test," Malvolio demands, "ask any reasonable question and I will answer it forthwith."

"Forthwith?" Feste says, pretending to be impressed. "Very well then. The ancient Roman, Pythagoras."

"—But Pythagoras was a Greek."

"—As I said," Feste comes back sternly, "in the opinion of the Greek Pythagoras, one's grandmother could be reborn as a bird. True or false?"

Malvolio is silent for a moment. "I have the highest respect for both grandmothers and birds—"

"True or false?" Feste raises his voice.

"False I would say. False!"

Feste pauses for effect. "—Then farewell! You must remain in darkness still. Before I could ever confirm that you've found your wits again, sir, you would have to accept the opinion of Pythagoras and be against the killing of birds lest you take the life of someone's grandmother. Farewell!"

"Stay, Father Topas!" Malvolio pleads in desperation. "*Stay!*"

But Feste has left and returned to Sir Toby and Maria by the stairs.

"Excellent, Father Topas," says Sir Toby, slapping him on the back and offering him a drink from the flask, which Feste declines, at least until he's got the beard off. "Su–perb," Sir Toby says, the last syllable of the word becoming a loud burp.

Maria scolds him with her eyes then looks to Feste. "You might have done it without the robe and beard," she snipes jealously. "He can't see you."

"Ah," Feste smiles at her, accepting the flask from Sir Toby, "but then it wouldn't have been any fun now, would it?" He sticks his tongue out at her then takes a drink.

"Go back and talk to him in your own voice," Sir Toby suggests, "then tell me what shape he is in." The effects of his drinking beginning to show, he stares morosely at his candle. "—If he can be freed without much ado, I would have it that way, and soon, for I'm so in the doghouse with my niece that this will prove the last straw. It's almost sure." He contemplates his candle in silence then looks to Feste. "I wish we were done with this…" Feste offers a sympathetic shrug and hands back the flask, Sir Toby putting it away, though not before having one last drink. "—Come to my room in a little while…" he says woozily, stumbling as he turns for the stairs, but Maria is there and steadies him from behind as he starts climbing...

"*Hey Robin, jolly Robin,*" Feste begins singing. "*Tell me how thy lady does...*"

"Fool?" Malvolio calls in the darkness.

"*My lady is unkind of late...*"

"Fool!"

"'*Alas, why is she so?*'"

"Fool, I say!"

"*Why, that's because she loves another now. —*Who calls there?"

"Good fool, if ever you want to earn my gratitude, help me get a candle, and a pen, and ink and paper. As I'm a gentleman, I promise I will be thankful to you for it."

"Master Malvolio?"

"Yes, good fool."

Picking up his candle, Feste goes back across the room and stands at the cell door. "Alas, sir, how did you come to lose your wits?"

"Fool, there never was a man so scandalously abused as me. I am as sound of mind as you are, fool."

"As sound of mind as me?" Feste laughs. "Then you're mad indeed if your mind is as sound as a fool's."

"They have locked me away, they keep me in darkness and send holy men to me, the asses—they do everything they can to drive me out of my mind."

"Watch what you say," Feste warns. "There is a holy man here." He puts on the voice of Father Topas. "*Malvolio, Malvolio, may heaven restore you to your sanity! Try to sleep, and above all, stop your infernal babbling.*"

"Father Topas—"

"*Don't talk with him, good fellow!*" Feste barks as Father Topas. "Who I, sir?" he asks in his own voice. "Not I, sir. God be with you, good Father Topas. "*—Indeed. Very well. Amen,*" he pronounces solemnly as Father Topas. "*—*I'll be careful, sir," he calls as if Father Topas is departing. "Believe me I will!"

"Fool, fool—fool, I say!" Malvolio cries in a frantic voice.

"Be patient, sir," says Feste, keeping his voice down. "There's serious trouble if I'm caught having words with you. What is it you want?"

"Just a light and some paper, and something to write with. I promise you I am as sane as any man in Illyria."

"Oh sir," Feste says with a sardonic smile, "if only you were…"

"I swear to you I am! Good fool, just fetch me what I need to write to my lady. It will be the most profitable letter you ever delivered."

"I will see if I can help you," Feste gives in. "—But tell me something first. Have you really lost your wits, sir, or is this but pretending?"

"—Believe me, sir, there is no pretense whatsoever."

Feste pauses in mocking contemplation of the request. "I should tell you I never believe a madman until I have proof that he's in his right mind…"

"I'll reward you more than handsomely, fool—just get going—please!"

Smirking and shaking his head, Feste starts back to the stairs. "I am gone, sir," he says in a mocking, singsong voice. "—But anon, sir, I'll return, sir, bringing what you need. Quick as I can, like the jester I am, your every plea I will heed—while *you* hold up your cross of wood, and shout at the devil, like a good madman should: *Be gone you devil, be gone!*" Reaching the stairs, he blows out his candle and goes up.

"Fool?" Malvolio calls out in the darkness….

Deep in thought, Sebastian is standing beside one of the fountains in Olivia's garden watching the play of afternoon sunlight on water, rainbows appearing in the clouds of spray caused by streams of falling water in the fountain pool below.

"This is the air," he muses to himself, "and these the rays of the sun. This pearl she gave me," he looks at it in the palm of his hand, "I can feel and see. Though I'm bewildered by the wonder of all that's happened," he glances away from the fountain, "yet I know it is not madness that has come over me." He starts along the path, something else weighing on his thoughts. "…And where is Antonio? I could not find him at The Elephant, although I was told he had been there before he went out again to search for me." He chuckles to himself. "—I wonder what he would have to say… Reason and my common sense tell me it could all be some mistake, but neither will let me believe it is madness that has befallen me." He takes in the colors and inhales the fragrance of the garden. "…Though too, this flood of good fortune so exceeds my wildest imaginings I wonder if I should any longer trust my eyes." He notices the sundial on its pedestal and walks over. "…Still, the power of reason persuades me this has nothing to do with madness. Unless, of course, my lady's mad," the thought occurs to him. "But if that were so," he reasons, "she could not manage her household and her servants with the confidence and grace I have seen her do." He laughs lightly, shaking his head. "Make of it what you will—"

"—I hope you can forgive me all this haste," Olivia pleads, coming up quickly behind him with a priest dressed in his robes. "—But if your intentions are as worthy as you profess, come with this holy man and me to the chapel hereby. There, in sacred presence, let us be made husband and wife, so my excited heart can be put at ease. We may keep it secret until such time as you wish to declare it true, and celebrate then as newly married couples joyfully do…"

"I'll follow this good man and go with you," Sebastian smiles, "and having sworn that I am yours, my vow will never prove untrue." He takes her hand gently and kisses it, Olivia meeting his eyes with an adoring smile when he looks up.

"Then lead the way, good father, and may the heavens always shine," she looks at Sebastian, "upon this blessed love of mine." Their faces are about to meet in a kiss when the priest clears his throat and gives a scolding frown, motioning them to be patient and follow him to the chapel….

The bells on his cap jingling wildly, Feste comes running down the path in Olivia's garden, Fabian in hot pursuit right behind.

"—If you were a good enough friend," he calls, "you'd let me see his letter!"

"Good Master Fabian," pants Feste. "Do me a favor first!"

"Anything!"

"—Don't ask to see this letter!" He tears past the sundial and darts behind the hedges to hide.

"You can't show the dog a bone then take it away!" Fabian hollers and slows up when he arrives at the sundial.

"Feste!" Fabian glances around—smiling a moment later when he sees the opening where he knows the fool has gone. He tiptoes stealthily toward it, rounds the hedge and jumps through.

"—Ah-ha!" he cries.

But there's no sign of the fool—only the sound of his feet on the other side of the hedge as he takes off, but along a different path. Bursting from behind the bushes, Fabian tears after him as far as the low stone fence at the end of the garden where it faces onto the street, just as Feste, flustered and out of breath, leaps to go over the fence— but he's too tired from running and his legs get tangled. He topples to the ground on the other side, losing the letter he's been carrying— which Fabian spots as he comes flying over the fence right behind him, scrambling to get his hands on the letter before Feste can.

"—Do you work for the Lady Olivia, friends?" a man's voice calls.

Reaching the letter first, Feste stuffs it in his pants and glances up to see Duke Orsino, Viola and an entourage of attendants, Curio and Valentine prominent among them.

"Indeed, sir," says Feste, still breathing hard and in no hurry to get to his feet, "we've been known to."

Leaning on the fence to get his breath back, Fabian sees Viola and scowls.

"—I met you before," Orsino says, smiling at Feste. "How are you, sir?"

"The better because of my enemies and the worse because of my friends," Feste gripes.

"You mean the better because of your friends..."

"No, sir," Feste disagrees, "the worse"

"How can that be?"

"Well sir," Feste offers and gets to his feet. "My friends call me a fool behind my back, whereas my enemies call me a fool to my face. At least with my enemies I know where I stand, while with my friends, I don't. And as long as I have legs, sir, I'll think it better to know where I'm standing, than where I'm not. Thus I say I'm *worse* because of my enemies."

"Excellent and clever!" the Duke applauds.

"In truth, sir, it's nothing much," Feste says dismissively, "though I hope I can count on *you* to treat me better than my friends."

"I wouldn't want you worse off because of me," Orsino comes back wryly and tosses him a gold coin. "Here's something for you...."

"Wouldn't a good friend make it two?"

"It's much cheaper being your enemy, fool," Orsino teases and tosses him another coin.

"Now, *three* is an interesting number, is it not sir?" Feste inquires hopefully, but the Duke shakes his head *No*: enough's enough.

"—Though if you can let your lady know I am here," he says, "and have her come and speak with me, it might reawaken my generosity."

"Indeed, sir," Feste winks, "may your generosity sleep well till I return. I go then, sir, yet I would not leave thinking my desire is that of a greedy man, sir." Orsino gives him a stare. "—But as you say, sir, let your generosity take a nap. I will awaken it soon." Back over the fence, he enters the garden and rushes off along the path, Fabian about to follow him when Viola speaks up.

"Here comes the man that rescued me, sir," she says to Orsino, pointing down the way where the two officers and their platoon of soldiers are returning to Olivia's, Antonio still their prisoner.

"That face of his I do remember well," says Orsino, watching the soldiers approach, "though when I saw it last, it was smeared black with the smoke and broil of battle. He was captain of a smaller vessel, not one to pose a serious threat, yet with a prowess that amazed our men he managed to destroy the finest ship in all our fleet, while we, begrudging him his victory, could only watch in awe and admiration as he sailed away unharmed. What's he done?"

"Not only the deed you speak of, sir," the first officer reminds the Duke, "but it was also this Antonio who took the *Phoenix* and her cargo as she returned from Crete. He is the one too who boarded the *Tiger*, when your young nephew Titus lost his leg. We arrested him here in the streets, brawling in defiance of your own decree forbidding it—"

"—I fought to save a citizen who'd been set upon by thieves," Antonio interjects in his own defense.

"He *did* do me a kindness, noble sir," Viola speaks up, "drawing his sword in my defense, though afterwards he did address me in the strangest sort of way—I knew not what he meant, nor if he might be mad."

The Duke turns his glance on Antonio. "Is this what thieves and pirates do to keep their reputation up? Return and taunt the enemy to its face?" He shakes his head in reproach. "Well, sir, it seems this foolish pride of yours has failed you after all."

"Noble sir," Antonio protests, "I take offence with what you've called me. Antonio has never in his life been either thief or pirate, although I will acknowledge having been Orsino's enemy years ago. As for my return, it was chance and, as I see now, unhappy circumstance that brought me to these shores again. I rescued from the storming sea that boy who now ungratefully stands beside you." He looks bitterly at Viola. "— Whipped by the wind and nearly drowned, he could barely cling to the timber on which he rode the cresting waves. There was little hope for his survival, but I tended him as if he were my brother, and coaxed him back to health without restraint or reservation, all in the name of friendship. It was for his sake, and my desire to be of further help to him, that I ignored the danger I knew I would be in the moment I set foot in this town. When earlier I saw him being attacked, I drew my sword and saved him even again, but in his treachery and cunning he made of me a stranger, and claimed he'd never seen my face until that very moment. He denied he'd ever known me, and refused to return the money I had given him an hour ago, to buy those things he needed for himself."

"How can this be?" Viola wonders to herself.

"—When did he come to town?" Orsino asks the first officer.

"Today, my lord," Antonio answers for himself, "yet we have been together day and night since I pulled him from the sea."

Orsino's face suddenly brightens—Olivia is making her way down the garden path toward them. "Here is the countess," he smiles and watches her approach, a number of her attendants in tow. "…Heaven walking on the earth," the Duke fawns under his breath, but then remembers Antonio. "As for you, sir," he says and turns, "I fear you must be mad. This fellow," he gestures at Viola, "has been with me for a few months now—though we'll talk of that later. Keep an eye on this man," he instructs the officers, who order the soldiers guarding Antonio to tighten their hold on the prisoner.

"—What is it you wish, my lord," Olivia says sharply as she arrives. "—Except for what you cannot have," she looks directly at him, "what is it you want from the Lady Olivia?" She darts her eyes at Viola just behind him. "—Cesario, you have broken your promise to me."

"Madam?" asks Viola with a puzzled frown.

"Gracious Olivia—" Orsino tries to speak.

"What do you say, Cesario?" Olivia presses, her eyes going back to the Duke while she waits for an answer.

"My lord would like to speak," Viola defers. "Duty compels me to keep silent."

"If it is the same old song, my lord," Olivia taunts Orsino, "all chorus, but no verse, you are wasting your breath, sir."

"Still so cruel," Orsino fumes.

"Still so faithful, my lord," Olivia comes back.

"To what, my lady, stubbornness? You callous woman, to whom

I've poured out the feelings of my heart—what shall be done with you?" he demands.

"What it pleases a man in your position to do," she counters, not missing a beat.

Incensed, Orsino glares bitterly. "Why shouldn't I—if I had the heart to—kill what I love so that none may have you in my place?" He pauses to regain his composure. "This is what I wish," he decides. "Since you disdain and spurn my feelings so—and since I know the one who takes my place in your affections—I'll see that you but waste away, the maiden with a heart of stone." He gives a gloating smile and puts an arm around Viola's shoulder. "I've come to esteem most highly this darling boy whom you adore." He keeps his eyes on Olivia. "I know I can never part with him, or let him stay a moment longer in your jealous sight." The matter settled, he turns to leave. "Come, Cesario, before my anger tempts me to something worse."

"Orsino!" Olivia calls to him.

"I'll sacrifice the one I love," he says blithely as he walks away, "to spite the raven's heart within this dove."

Viola prepares to follow the Duke. "Joyfully and willingly would I," she tells Olivia, "a thousand deaths for my Orsino die." She bows and starts along the path.

"Where are you going?" cries Olivia, trying to stop her.

Viola pulls away and continues walking. "—With him I love more than I love these eyes," she declares, "more than my life—more, by all the mores there be, than I will ever love a wife. And if it seems I but pretend," she calls back, "may the heavens above take my life for being false to the one I love."

"How you have wronged me Cesario—how cruelly misled me!" Olivia runs up and clutches at Viola from behind.

"*Who* misleads you, lady?" Viola turns around. "*Who* has done you wrong?"

"How can you have forgotten?" Olivia cries. "Has it even been that long? Bring the holy father here," she calls to one of her attendants who rushes off to fetch the priest...

Orsino has come back to Viola. "Cesario, we must away."

"No! Cesario—husband, stay!"

"Husband?" asks Orsino, astounded.

"Yes, husband," Olivia tells him, "which he dare not deny."

"Her *husband*, boy?" the Duke demands.

"—No my lord, not I."

"Only a fearful coward would say it is not so," Olivia pleads. "But worry not, Cesario dear. Take your life in your own hands now. Be true to what you know you are, and fortune will make you as great as him you fear." She casts a glance at Orsino whose eyes are on the attendant returning with the priest.

"—Welcome, Father," Olivia greets him warmly, but gets right to the point. "By your sacred duty, sir, tell the Duke what secret lies between this man and me."

The priest nods and offers a beatific smile.

"A contract of eternal love and joy," he says to Orsino, "—sealed by the joining of hands, a holy kiss, the exchange of rings, all verified and witnessed by myself not two hours past."

A stricken look on his face, the Duke turns on Viola. "I wonder what secrets else are hidden behind that loyal-seeming face..." He shakes his head in disgust. "One day you will trip yourself up with your bold conniving, Cesario—or whatever is your name. Farewell," he says and cast his eyes at Olivia. "Take her for your own, but make most sure our paths never cross again, for if I see you, I will end your life upon the spot."

"My lord, I swear—" Viola cries, distraught.

"—Don't swear," Olivia says, consoling, "you need not fear him any longer—"

"Someone call a doctor!" The voice of Andrew Aguecheek rings out behind them. His hat in one hand, the other holding a white handkerchief against the side of his head, he staggers up the path. "—He's cut me across the head and given Sir Toby a bloody wound as well. Help us, for the love of God!"

"What's happened?" Olivia cries.

"I wish I were at home instead of here," he mopes, taking the handkerchief away from his head to inspect it.

"—Who's done this, Sir Andrew?"

"The Count's attendant, the one named Cesario," he broods,

puzzled that his handkerchief isn't more stained with blood. "—We took him for a coward, but he's the devil and Satan combined!"

"My attendant Cesario?" Orsino asks.

Sir Andrew looks up and his eyes go wide when he sees Viola, thinking it's Sebastian. "God save me, it's him!" He puts the handkerchief to his head and takes a step back. "You wounded me for no good reason, sir!" he complains with an aggrieved tone. "I did what I did because Sir Toby put me up to it."

"Why do you accuse me, sir?" Viola comes back. "I never laid a hand on you. You drew your sword on me, in case you'd forgotten. I was polite and friendly—I certainly never hurt you."

"Then what do you call this?" Sir Andrew pouts and points to the handkerchief. "Apparently you think nothing of a bleeding head."

"Sir, I was never—"

"If Sir Toby hadn't been so drunk, he'd have beaten you much worse than he did."

Viola starts to reply, but everyone has turned at the sight of a drunk and limping Sir Toby, being helped along the path by Feste.

"Good sir," frowns Orsino and goes over to lend Feste a hand. "How are you doing, sir?"

" 'S nothing," Sir Toby snarls, though one of his pant legs has been cut open and blood is coming from inside. "—A scratch," he says, slurring the word badly. "Have you seen Dick the surgeon today?" he asks Feste.

"He's been drunk since eight this morning, sir. He's likely passed out by now."

"Then he's a *sot*, and a useless one at that. How I *hate* a drunken sot…"

"Take him inside," Olivia says with concern, several of her attendants hurrying to help with Sir Toby.

"I'll help you, Sir Toby," Aguecheek offers. "We'll have them treat our wounds together."

"*You'll* help?" Sir Toby says blearily as he sways on his feet, Feste, Sir Andrew and the attendants all working to hold him up. "What a trio it is—an ass, a fool and a dolt—a pasty-faced, empty-headed…" His voice trails off as he's led away.

"Get him to bed and see that his injury is treated!" Olivia calls after them, but while turning to speak with Orsino she starts when she sees— Cesario coming toward her from another part of the garden. She glances behind her at Viola standing with the Duke then casts her eyes at Viola's double: Sebastian.

"I'm sorry to have wounded your uncle, madam," he offers, walking up, "but had he been my own brother I could have done nothing else, I had to defend myself." He arrives beside Olivia and moves to take her hand but she pulls it back and stares. "Why do you look at me so strangely?" he asks. "Have I offended you by hurting your kinsman? Forgive me, sweet one," he pleads contritely, "and so soon after the vows I had made." He gets down on one knee and hangs his head, ashamed.

Like everyone else in the garden, Orsino is puzzled, glancing between Viola, who is standing beside him, and Sebastian, who is on bended knee before Olivia. "One face, one voice, one suit of clothes, but two people..." He stares at the uncanny resemblance between Viola and her brother. "—Is one of them real and the other not?" he asks, confounded.

Antonio, having spotted Sebastian, breaks free of his captors—the officers permitting his release, and he hurries forward, smiling at the sight of his friend.

"Antonio!" Sebastian calls. "How happy I am to see your face again!"

"But is it really you?" Antonio asks, suddenly not so sure.

"Of course it's me!" Sebastian tells him.

"But it's like you've been split in two—the halves of an apple couldn't be more alike than—" he casts his eyes at Viola. "Which one of you is the real Sebastian?"

"Most wonderful!" Olivia exclaims in disbelief.

Sebastian steps forward for a better look at Viola. "How can this be? I never had a brother, nor do I have the power to be in two places at once. I did have a sister, who was taken from me by the voracious sea. We must be related, sir, but how? Where are you from? What country? What name do you go by?"

"Sebastian of Messalina was my father's name," Viola answers, gazing at him bewilderedly. "Sebastian was my brother's name as well. He was dressed much like you are now when he was drowned. If spirits can take human form like this—surely that is why you have come, to torment us!"

"A spirit I may be, sir," Sebastian allows, "but one still clothed in the body he was born with. If you were not a man, though everything about you shows me you are, I'd shake my head and with tears coming on, say over and over 'Welcome, drowned Viola!'"

Still uncertain, she presses him for details. "My father had a mole upon his left brow."

"—So had mine."

"And my father died on Viola's thirteenth birthday."

"That day is etched forever in my memory," he says sadly. "He died but an hour after she was born."

"In place and time and circumstance, it seems we have good reason to be happy," she smiles. "You are who you claim to be, so let me prove the same. I'll take you to a captain from this town, at whose house are my woman's clothes. It's through his kindness I was saved, and came to serve this noble Count of Illyria, on whose behalf I visited this lady in hope that she would find a way to love him."

"—Then that is clearly how you were mistaken," Orsino tells Olivia. "But nature has seen to it that where you would have been married to a woman, you are now betrothed to a man." Olivia shoots him a look. "—But don't worry, fair lady," he teases, "in either case he'd have been of noble breeding" He laughs lightly at his own joke which, for the first time, Olivia finds amusing, and smiles. "Viola," he says and turns to her, "you have said to me a thousand times you would never love a woman as much as you loved me."

"And meant it in every word, and will gladly swear the same to you again, with all my heart."

"Give me your hand." Viola offers it to him. "Now let me see you in these woman's clothes that are with the captain who brought you here," he grins.

"I'm told he is in prison, noble sir, on a vicious accusation made by one Malvolio, a gentleman and steward to my lady."

"He shall be released," declares Olivia, without any hesitation, and soldiers dispatched by the officers march off to have the captain freed. "—Bring Malvolio here," she says to the last of her attendants who bows and goes. "Though now that I remember, he is said to have lost his wits." She looks away, reflecting. "His madness must have slipped my mind while dallying with it myself," she jokes dryly. "—How is he, sir?" she asks Feste, who along with Fabian, has come to join the group.

"As you might expect a man in his condition to be, madam," Feste allows. "He rails and curses at the devil hour by hour, although he has written you this letter. I should have given it over this morning, but as a madman's letters will hardly be the stuff of reason much less of gospel truth, I'd say it doesn't matter much when they end up getting delivered."

"Open it and read it."

"The words of a madman read by a fool," he snickers drolly and quips. " 'T will be enlightening if nothing else." He takes out Malvolio's letter, unfolds it and starts to read: "By the Lord, madam—" he shouts in a loud raving voice.

"What?" Olivia stops him. "Have you gone mad as well?"

"No, madam," Feste shrugs, "I'm only reading it so. If your ladyship wants to hear it as it sounds, you must let me do it in the man's own voice."

"I'd appreciate if you'd read it like you haven't lost your wits," she says firmly.

"I'm doing that, my lady. And I haven't lost my wits. But to read it like someone who *has*, is to read it the way I am. So pay attention, my princess, and listen up."

"You read it, sir," Olivia motions to Fabian.

With a gloating smile, he takes over reading the letter. " 'By the Lord, madam," he begins in a normal voice, "—you do me wrong and the world shall know of it. Although you have cast me into darkness and given your drunken uncle dominion over me, yet I am as fully in my senses as your ladyship herself. I have your own letter before me as I write, the one that caused me to behave to you as I did. With it I can put things to rights, and you will find yourself ashamed. Think what you will of me. I admit in saying this I am going against my duty to you, but I speak from a sense of profound injury to my person. The Badly Abused, Malvolio.'"

"Did he write this?"

"Yes, madam," Feste says.

"It doesn't sound like madness," the Duke observes.

"See that he's released, Fabian, then bring him here." He bows quickly to her and leaves. Olivia looks to Orsino. "My lord, I wonder would it please you—after giving the matter some thought—to think of me as a sister, now that my husband's sister will become your wife? And if it pleases you as well, let us have both weddings on one occasion, here in my house and at my expense."

"Madam," Orsino smiles, "I am happy to accept your offer—" he gazes at Viola, "if, for the service she has done him," he looks into her eyes, "so much against her will and woman's nature, but never doubting what would come to be—and all despite her own heart's strife, this prospective sister will consent before these friends, to be Orsino's loving wife."

"She will," Viola returns the Duke's smile.

"—Good God," Olivia says, alarmed.

"Is this the madman?" Orsino asks, he and Viola turning to see Malvolio storming through the garden ahead of Fabian.

"This is he, my lord—how are you Malvolio?" His clothes badly rumpled, his hair and clothes in disarray—the yellow stockings bunched around his ankles—he makes a sorry sight as he charges up and confronts Olivia.

"You have wronged me grievously, madam, grievously I say!"

"No—how have I done so, sir?"

"Lady, you have." He takes a letter from the inside pocket of his jacket and gives it to her. "You cannot deny it is in your handwriting." He folds his arms and taps his foot impatiently as Olivia peruses the letter. "You may object and claim the work is not your own: the handwriting not quite right, the phrasing a little off, and you might question whether the sealing wax or the paper are actually yours. But you can't dispute it, madam, so I seek the simple truth: why you would give me signs of favor clearly intended to show affection. And why," he harangues her, "you would order me to come to you smiling and cross-gartered in yellow stockings—have me be aloof with your uncle Sir Toby and the lesser people of your household. Yet when, in strict obedience, I acted on the words of your instructions, you had me confined in a very prison, kept me in a cold dark room where the parson came to visit me like one in jail—in short, madam, why you made of me a mocking spectacle, a laughing-stock, and a fool. Tell me why!"

"I am sorry, Malvolio," Olivia comes back patiently, "but I did not write this letter, though I would admit the hand is very like my own. I could guess and probably be right in saying Maria has penned these words—" she looks at it again and nods "—without question it is hers. And, come to think of it, it was she who first told me you were mad. Then you came to me all smiles, and pranced and cavorted, though not in ways suggested in the letter," she adds and gives him a smirking glance. "Please don't be upset with me. You were taken in a most malicious prank. And when we know why it was, and who the guilty parties were, you shall be the case's judge and jury."

"Good madam," Fabian pipes up beside her. "Permit me to speak, if you would, that no dispute or quarrel should mar the present joy amongst you here. Which to prevent I openly confess it was Sir Toby and myself who hatched the scheme to trick Malvolio—resenting his harsh and haughty treatment of us. Maria wrote the letter at the urging of Sir Toby, in return for which he's promised he will marry her. We thought our bit of mischief might provoke but mocking laughter that would teach the man a lesson, nothing more, when all is said and done."

"Indeed, poor fool," Olivia extends Malvolio her understanding, "their trick was most unkind."

"—'Some are born great,'" Feste snickers at him. "'Some achieve greatness, and some have greatness thrust upon them.'" Malvolio glares lividly. "—I confess to playing a part in this comedy myself," Feste acknowledges with a look to Malvolio, "as Father Topas, sir, though now, in truth, that's neither here nor there. "'By the Lord, fool, I am not mad.'" He laughs and shakes his head. "Remember, sir?" Malvolio sneers and looks away. "'Why the other day I saw him skewered by a street lackey.' Well, sir," Feste says, winking slyly, "what goes around, comes around."

"I'll be revenged on the lot of you!" Malvolio cries, incensed, and wheeling about, takes off toward the house.

"He *has* been grievously done by," Olivia sympathizes.

"Go after him," Orsino says to Fabian. "Talk to him and make your peace. He has yet to tell us of the captain who ran afoul of him. When that has been resolved and the long-awaited nuptial day arrives, marriage shall unite us all, our hands, our hearts, our lives." He turns to Olivia. "Meantime, sweet sister, we'll not depart just yet. Come, Cesario," he says with a kidding smile, "for as long as you're wearing the clothes of a man, I might as well continue addressing you as one. But when in woman's clothes you're seen, you'll be Orsino's love, his wife, his queen."

With the officers and soldiers returning to the street, Antonio joins Sebastian and Olivia, Viola and the Duke, and they move along the flowered path together, Fabian waiting for Feste, who takes his time and starts to sing:

"*A long time ago, when the world was young, with a hey, ho, the wind and the sun. Life was never so much fun—*"

"*But what does it matter?*" Fabian joins in. "*—When the story's over, the play is done!*" As he sings the last word, he snatches the cap from Feste's head, and tears off through the garden.

But Feste, knowing better, just shrugs to himself, and continues on his way....

New Directions

The Young and the Restless: *Change*

The Human Season: *Time and Nature*

Eyes Wide Shut: *Vision and Blindness*

Cosmos: *The Light and The Dark*

Nothing But: *The Truth in Shakespeare*

Relationscripts: *Characters as People*

Idol Gossip: *Rumours and Realities*

Wherefore?? *The Why in Shakespeare*

Upstage, Downstage: *The Play's the Thing*

Being There: *Exteriors and Interiors*

Dangerous Liaisons: *Love, Lust and Passion*

Iambic Rap: *Shakespeare's Words*

P.D.Q.: *Problems, Decisions, Quandaries*

Antic Dispositions: *Roles and Masks*

The View From Here: *Public vs. Private Parts*

3D: *Dreams, Destiny, Desires*

Mind Games: *The Social Seen*

Vox: *The Voice of Reason*

The Shakespeare Novels

Hamlet
King Lear
Macbeth
Midsummer Night's Dream
Othello
Romeo and Juliet
Twelfth Night

Spring 2008

As You Like It
Julius Caesar
Measure For Measure
Merchant of Venice
Much Ado About Nothing
The Tempest

www.crebermonde.com

Paul Illidge is a novelist and screenwriter who taught high school English for many years. He is the creator of *Shakespeare Manga*, the plays in graphic novel format, and author of the forthcoming *Shakespeare For the E-Generation*. He is currently working on *Shakespeare in America*, a feature-film documentary. Paul Illidge lives with his three children beside the Rouge River in eastern Toronto.